Sherlock Holmes and
The Deathly Clairvoyant

By

Margaret Walsh

First edition published in 2025
© Copyright 2025
Margaret Walsh

The right of Margaret Walsh to be identified as the author of this work has been asserted by her in accordance with the Copyright, Designs and Patents Act 1998.

All rights reserved. No reproduction, copy or transmission of this publication may be made without express prior written permission. No paragraph of this publication may be reproduced, copied or transmitted except with express prior written permission or in accordance with the provisions of the Copyright Act 1956 (as amended). Any person who commits any unauthorised act in relation to this publication may be liable to criminal prosecution and civil claims for damage.

All characters appearing in this work are fictitious. Any resemblance to real persons, living or dead, is purely coincidental. The opinions expressed herein are those of the author and not of MX Publishing.

Hardcover ISBN 978-1-80424-598-9
Paperback ISBN 978-1-80424-599-6
ePub ISBN 978-1-80424-600-9
PDF ISBN 978-1-80424-601-6

Published by MX Publishing
335 Princess Park Manor, Royal Drive,
London, N11 3GX
www.mxpublishing.co.uk

Cover design by Awan

In loving memory of my parents.

Chapter One

The paper today contained news about the rise of spiritualism as families seek solace from the terrible losses of what is now often termed "The Great War."

It is not the first time that this has happened. The words from the Bible: "The thing that hath been, it is that which shall be; and that which is done is that which shall be done: and there is no new thing under the sun," frequently come to mind.

The newspapers have taken to fulminating against mediums and séances, bemoaning that they are taking advantage of the suffering and sorrow of others.

I cannot help but think back to a strange case involving a family of mediums that Holmes and I were drawn into in the last decade of the 19th century.

I was back in my old rooms at Baker Street at the time, my wife having gone to the country to nurse a sick friend.

It was a chilly, blustery day in late October when Miss Kitty Pappwell came to our door seeking Holmes's assistance.

Mrs. Hudson showed Miss Pappwell to our rooms. "This is Miss Pappwell, Mr. Holmes," said Mrs. Hudson. "She has come to consult with you and Dr. Watson."

The lady would have been in her mid-to-late twenties. She was petite, standing around five feet and three inches tall. Miss Pappwell was well-dressed; stylish but not fashionable. Her hands were encased in soft leather gloves that I took to be made of the finest kid skin in a concession against the chill. She had fine blonde hair and blue eyes that gave her an almost doll-like appearance. It was an appearance only. Miss Pappwell's gaze was forthright as she looked from my friend to me and back again.

"Mr. Holmes," she said. "I wish to employ you."

Holmes gestured to her to take a seat. "In what capacity, Miss Pappwell? I warn you now, I do not involve myself with intrigues of the heart."

"Such intrigues do not concern me, Mr. Holmes. I wish for you to investigate a murder."

"That is surely the purvey of the police."

"It would be, Mr. Holmes, if the police believed it was murder."

"And they do not?"

Miss Pappwell shook her head. "No. They believe that my aunt committed suicide."

"And you do not?"

"No. My Aunt Amaryllis would not have done such a thing."

I opened my mouth to reply, but the lady cut me off.

"No, Dr. Watson. You must trust me on this. I know my aunt. We had made plans to visit an exhibition of the works of the artist Robert Anning Bell for the day after she died."

Holmes looked thoughtful. "I agree that it is unlikely that your aunt would have made such plans with you if she had intended to take her own life." He settled back comfortably in his seat. "Tell me everything, Miss Pappwell. Do not leave out a single detail, no matter how small."

"My aunt, Amaryllis Winterbottom, was the

widow of my mother's brother, Cornelius Winterbottom. Uncle Corny was a lawyer. He was a partner in the practice of Smythe, Hastings and Winterbottom in the City. When he died, Mr. Smythe and Mr. Hastings bought his share of the practice from Aunt Amy. This money, with what Uncle Corny had left her, enabled my aunt to live comfortably."

"Were there any children?" Holmes asked.

Miss Pappwell shook her head. "It was a great sadness to my aunt and uncle that they could not have children. My mother had eight children, of which I am number five. I gravitated towards my aunt at an early age. My mother considered me too free-spirited and too curious. Aunt Amy actively encouraged me to question the world around me."

"Who benefits from your aunt's death?" I asked.

"I do," Miss Pappwell replied. "I am my aunt's sole heiress."

"Tell me of the events that led up to your aunt's demise," Holmes said.

"My aunt had remained in the home that Uncle Cornelius had bought for them when he became a partner in the legal practice."

"Where is this house?" Holmes asked.

"It is close by Lincoln's Inn Fields. My aunt liked the bustle of London, and it was close enough to the City to be convenient for my uncle."

My friend nodded. "Pray continue."

"My aunt was much involved with good works, mostly to do with education. Being an educated woman herself, she felt that a good education gave a person an advantage in life. She never stopped learning. Aunt Amy was deeply interested in people. How they thought and why they did the things they do. You understand?"

Holmes nodded again. "Indeed, Miss Pappwell, the workings of the human mind are quite possibly the most interesting puzzle of all."

"My uncle died almost three years ago. About six months ago a friend of my aunt's suggested that she might like to visit a medium. She said that even if the medium was a fake and uncle did not make an appearance, it would be a good opportunity to observe."

"What did your aunt think of this?" I asked.

"She was quite taken with the idea of observing. Aunt Amy told me that she had no need to hear from Uncle Corney, but that her friend's suggestion had merit."

"The friend's name?" Holmes asked, motioning for me to make a note of it.

"Mrs. Felicity Hazelwick. They have been friends since they were young girls. I have her card in my bag." Miss Pappwell picked up her reticule and removed a card from it. I wrote down the Kensington address and handed the card back.

"My aunt began to ask around as to which medium would be good to visit. In the course of her enquiries, she came across the Loxworth family. They are something of a sensation, but unusual for clairvoyants, I am led to understand."

"In what way?" Holmes asked. "Pray forgive my ignorance, unless such people are outright frauds, they do not often come to my attention."

"That is understandable," Miss Pappwell said. "The clairvoyant mediums are three sisters. A set of twins and an older sister. They are managed by their brother. You commit to six sessions: two with each medium. The seances are held at the Loxworth home in Bloomsbury. A person may attend only six sessions. Repeat visits are forbidden. They will also not allow family members of former sitters to attend."

"I admit that that is indeed unusual," Holmes said. "I should have thought that, in the usual course of things, repeat visits would be encouraged. If only to fleece more money from the gullible flock."

Miss Pappwell raised her eyebrows. "You consider all clairvoyants to be frauds, Mr. Holmes?"

"Let us just say that in the course of my work I have never encountered a genuine one," Holmes replied.

Miss Pappwell nodded and returned to her story. "My aunt applied and was accepted. It was during her third séance that she learned why the Loxworths had become such a sensation."

"And why is that?" Holmes asked softly.

"One of the clairvoyants has a guide that comes through. Not at every séance, but at enough that his presence is feared."

"Feared? Why so?" I asked.

"They call him the Messenger of Death," Miss Pappwell replied. "And he comes through only to tell one of the sitters that they are going to die. Moreover, he always gives a date of death."

Holmes gave her a shrewd look. "And this messenger came to your aunt?"

"He did."

"And told her that she was going to die?"

"He did."

"And your aunt's reaction to this twaddle?"

"She laughed in the medium's face and stalked out of the séance. Aunt Amy sent for me the next day and told me what had happened. She refused to take it seriously. Indeed, she was scornful of the entire thing. That is when we made the arrangements to go to the exhibition."

"A brave woman," I commented. "I am not sure that I would have the courage to laugh in the face of someone who had prophesied my death."

"The day your aunt died?" Holmes asked softly.

"It was the day she was told it would be," Miss Pappwell responded flatly.

"How did your aunt die, Miss Pappwell?" Holmes asked.

"According to the police surgeon she drank poison. I am afraid that I do not know what poison. Which is why the police believe her death to be suicide. But they are ignoring several points that I have brought to their attention."

"And those points are?" Holmes asked.

"My aunt was found sitting in an armchair in her parlour. There was nothing near her that could have held poison. No cup. No glass. There is also a piece of jewellery missing. It is a tear drop ruby brooch that was one of the last gifts that Uncle Corney gave her."

Holmes sat in silence for a few moments. He looked across at the young woman. "Very well, Miss Pappwell, I shall take your case. I shall need from you a detailed description of the missing item, and your permission to access the house."

Miss Pappwell reached into her reticule again. "You have both, Mr. Holmes. I wrote out a description of the missing jewellery." She withdrew a sheaf of papers from the bag. "Here it is, along with the names of the police involved. I have included my own address as well. Please come to me when you wish to see the house. I have the keys."

Miss Pappwell paused, and then said, "I am afraid that I do not have details for the Loxworths. I know only that they live in Bloomsbury. There was nothing pertaining to them in my aunt's house. Not even a calling card."

"That is of no matter, Miss Pappwell. Such information can be easily acquired."

The young lady rose to her feet. "Thank you, Mr. Holmes. I am much reassured that there will be justice for my aunt with you taking the case."

"You are too kind, Miss Pappwell," Holmes murmured, as he showed the lady to the door.

Returning to our rooms he turned to me, a slight smile on his face, "Well, my friend, it looks as if, once again, the game is afoot."

I took my usual seat and looked up at my friend. "The Messenger of Death? You intend to take on the supernatural?"

Holmes waved his right hand in a dismissive gesture. "Bah! The Messenger of Death will prove to be mummery, no more than that. No, Watson, we are dealing with a very human murderer."

"How can you say that?"

"I am confident that if such a messenger from the divine or otherwise were truly making an appearance, then the deceased would not have been poisoned. Poisoning is such a prosaic way to die."

"You would expect something more theatrical?" I asked, amused despite myself.

"I would expect something a little less open to obvious murder," Holmes replied quietly.

I nodded. "What do we do first? Do we talk to the police officer in charge?"

Holmes consulted the papers that Miss Pappwell had given him. "I do not think so. The attending officer was Inspector Miles Lovell of E Division. I do not know the man. Let us not challenge his views until we have a little more to go on."

"That makes sense," I agreed.

"We need more information on Mrs. Winterbottom. I therefore suggest that we visit the offices of Smythe and Hastings, as well as the home of Mrs. Hazelwick. After that, I know someone who will mostly likely be able to assist us with the elusive Loxworth family."

I turned from where I was removing my coat from the stand to ask, "Your brother or Langdale Pike?"

"Well done, Watson!" Holmes said with a smile. "On this occasion, I think Langdale Pike would be more useful. Unless the Loxworths are a threat to Queen and country, I very much doubt Mycroft will have expended the energy to have them watched."

Chapter Two

The offices of Smythe and Hastings were located in Took's Court, just off Cursitor Street. The narrow court had quite a history. It had been home to the novelist Charles Dickens when he was a parliamentary journalist. Dickens had inserted the street into his novel *Bleak House*, immortalizing it as 'Cook's Court.'

The court was clean and swept clear of rubbish and the steps up to Smythe and Hastings were well scrubbed.

A well-dressed young man answered our ring and, upon hearing of our errand, escorted us to a small withdrawing room just inside the front door.

He disappeared further into the building. A few minutes later an older man appeared in the doorway. This man was tall and spare, with dark hair that was greying at the temples. His keen grey eyes swept over us both. "Mr. Holmes? Dr. Watson? Jeremy tells me that you wish to speak with us about the Winterbottoms?"

"That is so, Mr...?"

"Anthony Smythe, at your service," the man replied, holding out his hand for us to shake. "Come, gentlemen, we shall have this meeting in Lawrence's office."

Mr. Smythe escorted Holmes and me up a flight of stairs and into a spacious office with windows that overlooked the court below. Beneath one of the windows was a large mahogany desk behind which another man was sitting.

This man, who introduced himself as Lawrence Hastings, was as tall as Mr. Smythe and about the same age, but there the resemblance ended. Hastings was fair-haired, blue-eyed, and leaning towards corpulence.

As we were seated, Mr. Hastings said, "I am curious as to why the detective, Mr. Sherlock Holmes, wishes to talk to us about our late partner and his wife."

"You are aware of Mrs. Winterbottom's death?" Holmes asked.

Both men nodded solemnly. "A tragedy," Hastings said quietly. "We exerted quite a great deal of effort to ensure that Amaryllis was buried beside her husband."

Smythe frowned, "The vicar was most obdurate about having a suicide buried in hallowed ground."

Holmes raised an eyebrow. "He cannot have been that obdurate if you succeeded."

Smythe gave us a wintry smile. "Men of the church are as susceptible to bribery as any other. In this case the offer to replace the cushions on the pews was sufficient to engage his Christian charity."

"Mrs. Winterbottom's niece came to me," Holmes said softly. "She does not believe that her aunt committed suicide."

Hastings smiled fondly, "Little Miss Kitty-Kat would not. Such a charming child. Cornelius would bring her with him to work some days." He looked sharply at Holmes. "As well as being a charming child, Kitty was also a clever one. I doubt that she has lost that cleverness as a woman. She would not have gone to you if she did not believe you could help."

Smythe leaned forward in his chair. "Kitty must know something the police do not."

"The police know it," Holmes said, "…but have dismissed it. You are aware of the manner of death?"

Both men nodded again. "Poison," Smythe said.

"Indeed. However, there was no sign found of how the poison was administered."

"Do you know what the poison was?" Hastings asked?

Holmes shook his head. "No. Miss Pappwell did not know, and I have yet to approach the police for a copy of the report."

Smythe shook his head. "I am sure you have someone who would get it for you, but would you allow me to do this?"

Holmes gave the man a thoughtful look. "If you wish to. May I ask why?"

Smythe paused for a moment, clearly gathering his thoughts. "It seems to me, Mr. Holmes, that we wrote poor Amaryllis's death off as suicide without thinking it through. Lawrence and I owe it to both Amaryllis and Cornelius to assist you."

"Was Mrs. Winterbottom's demeanour such that

you readily accepted the verdict of suicide?" I asked.

Both men fell silent. "No," Hastings said at last. "It had been several years since Cornelius's death. Amaryllis missed him, but she was enjoying life as a respectable widow." He looked up sadly. "We are lawyers. We should have known something was not right about her death."

"Mr. Holmes," Smythe said. "Whatever fee you are charging, please give the bill to us, not Miss Pappwell."

Holmes nodded and got to his feet. I followed suit.

"Thank you for your time, gentlemen. I look forward to receiving the post-mortem report in due course."

Smythe nodded. "I shall personally bring it to Baker Street when I obtain a copy."

Holmes nodded his thanks, and we took our leave.

"Where to next, Holmes?" I asked when we were out in the street. "Mrs. Hazelwick?"

Holmes nodded as he flagged down a cab for us, and, having given the cabbie the address, settled back in his seat.

"Do you think the lady will be able to help?" I asked.

Holmes shook his head. "If you mean material help, then no. But, according to Miss Pappwell, Mrs. Hazelwick was the person who raised the idea of seances with Mrs. Winterbottom. If nothing else, I would like to know why."

I nodded and settled back into the seat and amused myself watching London go by the window.

Chapter Three

Mrs. Hazelwick lived in a fashionable part of Kensington, close by Kensington Palace and the park.

A smartly dressed maid answered the door and escorted us into a comfortable parlour. Four well-stuffed armchairs sat around a largeish occasional table in the centre of the room. A beautifully carved oak bookcase sat against a wall. Several matching wall cabinets, containing what appeared to be Sevres porcelain, decorated the walls. On the wall above the mantelpiece was a painting of a god chasing a startled nymph that looked as if it had been painted by the pre-Raphaelite artist Edward Burne-Jones. This was not a household that was short of money.

Mrs. Hazelwick came hurrying in, followed by the maid pushing a tea trolley containing a fine china teapot with matching cups and saucers, and several plates containing caraway seed biscuits, honey cake, and what looked to be a very fine gingerbread.

Once we had been served with tea and comestibles, our hostess took her seat and smiled at us both. "I see that Kitty has done what she said she would do and engaged you to investigate Amy's death."

"Do you agree with her course of action, ma'am?" Holmes asked.

"Oh yes," the lady said firmly. "There is no way that Amaryllis Winterbottom would kill herself. The very idea is preposterous. I told that jumped-up police detective so. The cheek of the man. Seeing a woman dead of poison and immediately saying it was suicide."

"The police detective in question being Inspector Miles Lovell?" Holmes asked.

"Yes, Mr. Holmes. Such an impertinent man. Old enough to know better as well." She stuck her nose in the air and made her voice a little gruff, "I am a police officer, madam. I know about such things. Run along now."

I hid a smile behind my teacup.

Holmes chuckled dryly. "There are many police officers like him, I am afraid." He set his cup down on the table. "Tell me, Mrs. Hazelwick, what made you suggest spiritualism to Mrs. Winterbottom."

"Well, Mr. Holmes, Amy was always interested in people. Who they were, and, especially, why they did things. She was always looking for something new to examine. I had read in the newspaper about how people were consulting mediums to contact their deceased loved ones. I showed the article to Amy."

"What did Mrs. Winterbottom say about the article?" Holmes asked.

"She laughed and said that people were fools chasing after shadows. She did, however, agree that it would be a fine situation to observe other people in."

"Did you suggest the Loxworth family to her?" I asked.

Mrs. Hazelwick shook her head. "Oh no, Dr. Watson. Amy found them all by herself. I do not know how. She told me a couple of weeks after our discussion that she had found a séance group to attend."

"Did she tell you about the Messenger of Death?" Holmes asked.

Mrs. Hazelwick nodded. "Yes. After the creature prophesied her death."

"What was Mrs. Winterbottom's reaction to that?" Holmes asked.

"She laughed, Mr. Holmes. She laughed." Mrs. Hazelwick gave us a sad smile. "It looks as if the last laugh was on her. Poor Amy." Mrs. Hazelwick's eyes filled with tears, and I hastened to fetch the maid.

Leaving the lady in the care of her maid, Holmes and I quietly took our leave.

Our next port of call was a gentleman's club in St. James Street. This was the home and office of the gossip-columnist Langdale Pike.

As we approached the club, Pike could be clearly seen ensconced in the club's bow window. He was obviously hard at work. Notebooks and papers were strewn across the table that served as his writing desk and the man himself was studying what appeared to be a letter and making notes in one of his notebooks.

Langdale Pike did not look up as we walked past the window and up the front steps. Nevertheless, I was certain that the man had seen us.

A liveried footman let us into the club and, when Holmes told him our business, escorted us to where

Langdale Pike sat.

Pike smoothly pushed his papers to one side of the table and rose to his feet to greet us. "Sherlock!" he said with a smile. "And Dr. Watson! What interesting case brings you to me?"

We sat in the chairs that the footman had provided, and then Pike waved the man away, instructing him to bring coffee and cake for us all.

Once the refreshments had been served and the footman had retreated out of listening range, Holmes began to tell Pike what had happened.

Pike listened carefully and in silence until Holmes had finished. He then leaned back in his chair; his expression thoughtful.

"I have heard of the Loxworth family. There are four of them. Three sisters and their brother. The young women are the clairvoyants. The brother is their manager. They live in Bloomsbury. And that, my dear Sherlock, is about the extent of my knowledge of them."

"They have not come to your professional attention?" Holmes asked.

Pike shook his head. "Their paths do not usually cross with those who appear in my columns. In fact, they appear to go out of their way to avoid contact with the aristocracy. Which is odd, because most of their sort crave aristocratic patronage. It makes their path a lot smoother."

Pike frowned. "However, I do believe that I know someone else who may be able to help you. He is a member of this club."

"And that would be?" Holmes asked.

"Major Donald Porthey. He is a member of the S.P.R."

"What on earth is the S.P.R.?" I asked.

According to Pike, the S.P.R. or Society for Psychical Research was a foundation started in 1882 by William F. Barrett, an English scientist who became interested in researching the occult and uncanny after an encounter with mesmerism in the 1860s.

The S.P.R. had been formed to investigate all aspects of the occult, centring, for the main part, on mediums and poltergeist phenomena. The founding members had been quite illustrious, including Henry

Sidgwick, the Knightsbridge Chair of Moral Philosophy at Cambridge; and the poet and philologist, Frederic W. H. Myers. Other members of the society included Charles Dodgson, who was better known to most people by his pseudonym of Lewis Carroll; as well as Alfred, Lord Tennyson; and the writer Arthur Conan Doyle.

Holmes left a message with Langdale Pike to pass on to the major, and we took our leave.

Once outside, I turned to Holmes. "Where to now, Holmes?"

"I think, my dear Watson, that it is time we paid Miss Taverner a visit. That admirable lady may have heard something."

Miss Cynthia Taverner was a private enquiry agent that Holmes and I had worked with in the past. The charming young woman ran her own agency from an office in Jermyn Street.

The office of Taverner's Private Enquiries was staffed by a jovial middle-aged man with fading red hair. This was Robert Boscombe, Miss Taverner's clerk. The role of clerk to a detective was the perfect role for Mr. Boscombe. The man was a crime enthusiast who delighted in my stories in the *Strand Magazine* and was a regular reader of the notorious *Police Gazette*. The man in question rose, smiling, from his desk when we entered.

"Mr. Holmes. Dr. Watson. A pleasure to see you both again."

"A pleasure to see you again, Mr. Boscombe," I said, knowing Holmes's tendency to simply ignore pleasantries if they consumed too much of his time. "We would like to speak with Miss Taverner if she is in."

Boscombe fairly beamed. "Miss Taverner is always in for you gentlemen."

He hastened to a door that was set in the wall directly behind his desk and knocked. Opening the door, he stuck his head into the room beyond and said, "Mr. Holmes and Dr. Watson are here to see you, Miss Taverner."

Cynthia Taverner came to the door and escorted us into her office. Miss Taverner was a pretty young woman, with dark hair, merry brown eyes, and a dimple in her cheek that flashed when she smiled.

Miss Taverner's office was slightly smaller than the outer one. One window, set high in the wall, looked down into the small, dusty, back yard of the tailor's shop below. A well-polished oak desk with a matching chair sat before the window. Bookcases were set against the walls, interspersed with several solid filing cabinets made of oak. On the wall next to the window hung a portrait of a man: Frederick Taverner.

Frederick Taverner, M. P., was Cynthia's cousin. The inclusion of his portrait in her office was, I thought, a nice touch to let prospective clients know that the lady had the right connections for the job. I mentally applauded her perspicacity.

Cynthia led Holmes and I to two comfortable chairs set before the desk. Boscombe was sent for coffee for us all, and when we each had a cup, Cynthia seated herself behind her desk and looked at us. "What brings you to my office, gentlemen?"

Taking a sip of his coffee, Holmes, once again, related the story told to us by Miss Pappwell. Cynthia listened with keen interest.

Once Holmes had finished, she sat back in her seat, her expression thoughtful.

"It sounds almost fantastical," Cynthia finally said. "Like something out of one of Edith Nesbit's dreadful tales."

While best known for writing charming tales for children, Edith Nesbit was also a writer of stories for an adult audience. Many of these stories were tales of true horror. Her story *The Ebony Frame* had cost me a night's sleep.

"I have heard nothing about the Loxworths," Miss Taverner said. She looked thoughtful. "I do, however, have one or two friends who move in such circles. I shall contact them and see what I can find out." Cynthia paused. "Have you considered talking to Dorothy Watts?"

"I had not," Holmes said. "The lady is busy with her work for my brother."

"As I have been recently," Cynthia said with a slight smile. "But Dorothy certainly has some interesting contacts."

I could not forebear smiling. Dorothy Watts was

a young friend of ours who now worked for Mycroft Holmes. She had brought us useful information in several cases and had taken part in some herself. Indeed, I owed my life to her. She saved me during the course of the case that I have written up elsewhere as *The Molly-Boy Murders*.

Holmes acknowledged that Miss Taverner was most likely correct.

Having appraised the lady of the case and elicited her agreement to keep an ear out for any information that might be useful, Holmes and I took our leave and returned to Baker Street.

On our return to our rooms, we discovered that Major Porthey had already been and had left his card saying he would return that evening.

Holmes held the card in his hand and looked at me. "You can say what you like about Langdale Pike, my dear Watson, but you must admit that he is a swift worker."

I admitted that this was so and sat down to write up my notes on the case so far, such as they were.

Chapter Four

It was about 7 p.m. when we heard a knock on the front door, followed by the voice of Billy the page boy, and that of a man.

This was followed by heavy, but halting, footsteps on the stairs. There was a peculiar tap with each step that was, I realized, the sound of a walking stick. I was not, therefore, surprised when the major came into our rooms using a cane.

What I was surprised by was his relative youth. Being a major, I was expecting a much older man, but this gentleman was only in his forties. He was tall, with the squared shoulders of a military man. His hair was dark and sleek, and he sported a well-groomed moustache. The cane he leant upon was of smooth, well-polished ebony, with a carved silver handle.

He nodded his head to us. "Good evening, gentlemen, Major Donald Porthey at your service. Langdale Pike gave me your message. I admit that I am intrigued as to why the famous Mr. Sherlock Holmes wants my help."

"Take a seat," Holmes said. "And we will tell

you what is happening. But first, maybe a drink?"

"A whisky, if you have it, would be very pleasant this cold evening," the major replied.

I got up from my seat and hurried to the cabinet where we kept our alcohol. We had several bottles of extremely good Scots whiskies that had been gifts from wealthy clients. I poured a generous measure of *Royal Lochnagar* into a class and handed it over. Our guest having indicated as I poured that he did not take water in his whisky.

Major Porthey took a sip and smiled appreciatively.

"How did you become interested in the S.P.R.?" I asked. "It seems a strange interest for a retired military man."

Porthey smiled slightly. "No more so than chronicling the cases of the world's first consulting detective, Captain Watson."

I laughed and shook my head. "A purely nominal rank. I had no military power. The rank is a courtesy only." I looked at our guest with some amusement. "As I believe you well know."

Major Porthey raised his glass to me. "That I do. Though when you are injured you believe every army surgeon has power next only to that of God himself. Especially if you try to leave your bed before they are willing to let you." He took another sip of his drink, and looked at us thoughtfully. "To understand why I joined the S.P.R. you really need to know how I came to be invalided out of Her Majesty's army."

I got Holmes a drink of brandy and took a glass of the *Royal Lochnagar* for myself, then we settled back to listen.

"I served in the Third Burma War," Major Porthey said. "Not the actual war itself. That only lasted twenty-two days."

The somewhat misnamed Third Burma War had occurred in 1885 when Great Britain, annoyed by French and Chinese meddling in a region they considered their own particular sphere of influence, invaded Burma. The excuse, that some consider spurious, came after a British company, the Bombay Burma Trading Corporation, was accused of under-reporting its export of the highly prized wood, teak, and of not paying its employees. Fines were levied and the British government accused the Burmese courts of corruption and demanded that a British arbitrator be appointed to the case. When the Burmese quite naturally refused, an ultimatum was issued on the 22nd of October 1885. An ultimatum that would have restricted the Burmese government to little more than figurehead status. Reducing the country to the same level as many of the Indian states. Nominally headed by a prince but, in actuality, led by the British. Of course, the Burmese refused again.

On the 9th of November 1885, it was decided to occupy the city of Mandalay and dethrone King Thibaw Min. The part of the whole expedition that caused much disapproval in certain circles was the proclamation circulated amongst the Burmese people that the aim of the invasion was to place Prince Nyaungyan, the older half-brother of Thibaw Min, and one of the few siblings to escape Thibaw Min's murderous spree upon his accession, to the throne. This of course, had the effect of lowering resistance from the general Burmese population. The only problem with the plan was, as our government knew full well, Nyaungyan was already dead. He had died in exile in India. All in all, the Third Burma War was a sordid little tale of governmental greed and arrogance.

Major Porthey continued, "I am sure you are aware that though the war was effectively over in twenty-two days, pockets of resistance remained."

That was something of an understatement. The Burmese people fought a furious running battle against the British of the type now known as "guerrilla warfare." A term which arose during the Duke of Wellington's campaign during the Peninsular War in the early part of this century where groups of Spanish and Portuguese partisans called *guerrilleros* helped drive the French out of the Iberian Peninsula.

"The natives fought fiercely," Major Porthey continued. "They were relatively well-armed. We could never find out where the guns were coming from. To my mind the most likely case was that they were being smuggled across the border from India. We British are not universally popular there."

Holmes and I made faint noises of agreement.

The major carried on. "It became necessary to send regular patrols out of the cities to remind the natives that we were in control. My patrol was near a village where there had been a lot of anger but had seemed to settle down and accept the British presence. So, we decided to visit to show the flag, so to speak." Porthey took a sip of his whiskey. "There was an explosive device set in a small pile of rocks near the entrance to the village. It went off just as we went through the gates. Several of my men were injured, some were killed, and I got a piece of scrap metal in my knee." Porthey pulled a face. "The village was deserted. The inhabitants had melted into the jungle leaving the bomb as a farewell gift to us. I spent weeks in hospital, but it became obvious that I would not walk properly again, so I was invalided out. Sent back to India and thence back here."

Porthey took another sip of his whisky. "It was when I was in India before coming home, that I got this stick." He held out his walking cane for our inspection. As I had noted, it was made from ebony, but I had been unable to see the handle clearly before. The handle was of silver and engraved with several symbols. Though I had not been long in India, I recognised them as Hindu.

"The stick was a gift from a wealthy Indian merchant with whom I had formed a friendship. He was the bastard son of a prince, but had been treated well by his father, having been educated in England."

"At the same school you attended," Holmes said.

Porthey nodded. "Bhavesh is a good sort. He was horrified when I came back from Burma injured. He had this stick made for me. The handle is solid silver, and the engravings are all symbols of protection of their god Vishnu. It was this stick that led me to the S.P.R."

"How?" I asked, by now deeply curious.

"On the ship home was a retired reverend gentleman who had been in India visiting his son. He spotted the engravings on my stick and struck up a conversation."

"Odd behaviour for an Englishman," Holmes observed. "And a retired churchman at that."

Porthey chuckled. "True. The fact is he thought that he and I shared an interest because of the symbols on my stick."

Holmes leaned forward to study the stick. Porthey obligingly held it out so that my friend could examine the handle.

Porthey continued. "The symbols are those of the god Vishnu and are for protection. One of them is the Kaumodaki." He pointed to an elaborate mace that was the main decoration down the shaft of the handle. "It provides protection against evil spirits, amongst other things."

Holmes hummed. "Therefore, the reverend gentleman thought you shared his interest in ghosts and suchlike and had obtained some protection."

Porthey laughed. "He did. The poor chap was somewhat embarrassed to have misjudged the situation. However, I was bored, so I asked him to tell me about his interest. I was expecting to be told ridiculous ghost stories, but what I learned instead was how the society investigates hauntings and mediums. Trying to find evidence of such things, but many times just as content to expose frauds preying on the desperate."

"You were interested," I said.

"I was," Porthey agreed. "So much so that when an offer was extended to attend a meeting and possibly become a member, I accepted. I have a little money so that, with my army pension, I can afford not to work. Not that there is much work to be had for a man who does not have full use of all his limbs."

The last was all too true. There were far too many men severely injured or missing limbs from Great Britain's many military forays abroad who were reduced to begging in the streets. The military pension was not much for an officer; it was even less for enlisted men, who were cast aside when they could no longer serve.

"I found that most of the members of the S.P.R. are men with a scientific turn of mind, much like you, Mr. Holmes." Porthey nodded to my friend. "I freely admit that I was expecting to meet charlatans and was pleasantly surprised when I did not. Not all of the investigations interested me. I found that I was most interested in hauntings of places and in poltergeist visitations. Both, I think, can be more easily scientifically measured and tested."

Holmes nodded his approval of the major's attitude. "Will you be able to help us with our case?"

Porthey nodded again. "I will. Lord Peter gave

me your message."

I admit I was bewildered. "Lord Peter?" I asked, not recalling meeting anyone of that name.

"Langdale Pike," Holmes replied. "It would not do to use his real name. He is a younger brother of the Duke of Denver."

I blinked in astonishment, and Porthey continued. "I am told you are interested in the Loxworth sisters?"

"We are," Holmes replied.

"In that case, I think I can point you in the direction of someone who can assist. I know two of our members have evinced an interest in them. I shall contact them on your behalf and bring them around, if that suits you?"

"That suits very well," Holmes replied.

"Excellent." Porthey got carefully to his feet, using his cane for balance. "Thank you, gentlemen, for inviting me, and for the excellent whisky. I shall be in contact shortly." Nodding to us, the major took his leave.

To our surprise, no sooner had the major left, than the lawyer, Anthony Smythe, arrived.

"Pray forgive me for coming this late, gentlemen," were his opening words. "I managed to obtain the post-mortem report only this evening and did not want to wait until tomorrow to deliver it."

Holmes was all affable charm. "Not at all, Mr. Smythe, so good of you to put yourself out on our behalf."

Smythe declined my offer of a drink but settled himself into a chair as Holmes eagerly read the few sheets of paper that clinically chronicled the death of Amaryllis Winterbottom.

"Hmmm. All fairly straightforward. Woman of middle years. Blood pooled in the buttocks and thighs. Lungs completely deflated. Ah! Here we are! Liquid remains found in the stomach. Well, well, well. What do you make of this?" Holmes handed the report to me.

I skimmed down until I reached the section about the liquid and then I stopped and stared. "Traces of atropine, hycosine, and hyoscyamine? What on

Earth? All of these are plant poisons!"

"Exactly, my dear Watson. And, more importantly, they can all be found in one plant – henbane. Also known as Black Henbane. Its scientific name is *Hyoscyamus niger* of the *Solanaceae* family. The collapsed lungs, along with the three toxins, seals it. The poison has to be henbane. In the hands of a skilled medical man, the plant is hugely beneficial. In the hands of an amateur it can be deadly. In the hands of a murderer, it is the almost perfect poison."

"Almost perfect?" Smythe asked.

"Unlike many other poisons, it does not cause vomiting. It has been used medically for centuries. Legend has it that simply smelling the flowers can cause drowsiness. Henbane has been used to aid sleep, to ease toothache, and to calm digestive disorders."

"But it is deadly," Smythe said.

"So is opium," Holmes retorted. "So are many other drugs. In the hands of skilled professionals, like my friend here, there is no problem. And in the case of henbane, it grows wild. Our murderer could easily have picked it in a park. Though, it is more likely that our killer is cultivating his own. Otherwise, he would have to rely on chance when he wanted to kill. And this killer is too canny to rely on the unreliable."

"But it definitely is murder?" Smythe asked.

"I cannot see it being anything else," my friend replied. "For those suicidally inclined, the poison of choice tends to be laudanum, which can be legally obtained, and most households have a bottle. Even arsenic is readily available. Henbane is not so easy to get in this city. It grows in well-drained and sunny places, something that is in short supply in London. The plant also prefers chalk or sandy soils. While there is some chalky soil in London, most of London's soil is clay based. It does grow here but it is not as prevalent as in some other places. It grows quite well in Kent, I believe, as well as Dorset and Wiltshire."

Anthony Smythe got to his feet. "I leave the report with you, Mr. Holmes, and I thank you for the opportunity to aid in finding poor Amy's killer. You will let us know what happens?"

Holmes nodded. "I assure you, Mr. Smythe, that you will be fully informed as to the outcome."

"Thank you, Mr. Holmes. Lawrence and I owe Amy that. As my partner stated, we are lawyers. We should have known something was wrong about her death."

"Do not belabour yourselves over it," Holmes advised. "It will do you no good. Her death is being properly investigated now. That is the main thing."

"You are correct, Mr. Holmes." Anthony Smythe nodded to us. "Goodnight, gentlemen."

Anthony Smythe took his leave and, standing at the window, I watched him walk down Baker Street to hail a cab.

I turned back from the window towards my friend. "What now, Holmes?"

"Now? Now we wait."

"For another death?"

"I hope not. For I have no way of knowing whom the possible victim may be. No, my dear Watson, we wait for Major Porthey to bring his colleagues to us."

"It seems that all we are doing with this case is

waiting," I observed.

"It does seem that way," Holmes agreed. "Goodnight, Watson." Holmes turned to head to his room.

"Goodnight, Holmes," I replied, as I turned back to the window to gaze out at the darkened street below.

Chapter Five

We did not have to wait too long. Major Porthey sent a message around the next morning advising that he had spoken with his colleagues, and they were amenable to meeting with us. Holmes wrote back extending an invitation for that afternoon.

Advised that we were having guests, Mrs. Hudson went into a flurry of baking. The delightful, sweet, scent of hot baked goods floated upstairs to our flat.

Major Porthey arrived promptly at 3 p.m., accompanied by two gentlemen who were introduced as Andrew Thornwood and Jonathan Harbury. The latter name seemed vaguely familiar to me, though I could not recall meeting anyone of that name.

I helped Mrs. Hudson set the table for tea. In addition to the well-used, fat, brown teapot, a pot of coffee was provided as well as milk, cream, and sugar. Plates of tongue and pickle sandwiches, ratafia biscuits, plum cake, lavender shortbread, and spice biscuits joined them on the table. It was a goodly spread, and I noticed our visitors eyeing it keenly.

I poured tea for our visitors and myself and coffee for Holmes, before gesturing to everyone to help themselves to comestibles.

As we were eating, Major Porthey outlined his one of his colleague's credentials. Andrew Thornwood turned out to be a member of the clergy. The Reverend Andrew Thornwood was in his forties. Of average height, Thornwood had dark, straight hair that was greying at the temples.

"How does a man of the cloth come to join the Society for Psychical Research?" I asked.

He took a sip of his tea. "I became interested after I was asked to perform an exorcism at an old house in my parish. Officially the church does not perform such rites. It is considered theatrical nonsense, more in keeping with the Roman church. But, as a man of God, I felt I had to do something, even if it were just to be a comforting presence. A couple of members of the Society were also present. I found the whole thing very interesting and went to a few meetings. I formally joined around about the same time as Porthey here."

"And your superiors in the church do not mind?"

Holmes asked.

"It is one of the quirks of the Church here in England," Thornwood replied, "…that belief in God is preferable, but not essential." Thornwood smiled briefly to show he was joking. "My bishop evinced the opinion that it was frankly much better than the interests of one of my colleagues in a neighbouring parish. He collects coprolites. The bishop said he hates visiting because the man's study is lined with glass cases filled with fossilized faeces. At least my study has books."

He smiled at the third member of the trio. "Harbury here was a member before both of us. We have found that we work well together."

"We do indeed," the other man replied. He was older than Thornwood, being somewhere in his fifties. His hair was iron-grey, and his blue eyes twinkled with good humour. "Between Thornwood's book learning and my stage-smarts, very few frauds get away from us."

"Of course!" I exclaimed. "You are the 'Amazing' Jonathan Harbury, the stage magician."

"Retired now, my dear sir. But it is kind of you to recognise me. In my day I performed feats on stage that many fraudulent mediums still use. That knowledge helps me to catch them out. It is one thing to use such tricks to entertain upon the stage. The people coming to see such a show are expecting something wondrous and beyond belief." Harbury's expression darkened. "But to use such tricks to con money from the grieving and the vulnerable, well, that is a different proposition entirely. I became interested in the Society after I was asked to assist with outing a fraudulent medium. I found the whole thing interesting and, frankly, retirement was very dull."

Harbury had been a major music hall attraction for quite a number of years. He had been compared, favourably, to the great John Nevil Maskelyne, arguably Britain's greatest stage magician.

Harbury turned his attention to Holmes. "Porthey tells us that you are interested in the Loxworths."

"We are," Holmes replied. "We have a client, the niece of one of their…" He paused, clearly looking for the right word.

"The word 'sitter' is the word you are looking for," Thornwood said quietly.

"Thank you, Reverend. The niece of one of their sitters is our client. Tell me, gentlemen, have you ever heard of the Messenger of Death?"

Thornwood tilted his head thoughtfully. "I cannot say that I have. The Bible mentions the Angel of Death, but not the Messenger."

"The Messenger of Death comes through them and tells one of the sitters that they are going to die and then names the date."

"What?" Harbury stared at my friend, aghast. He turned to Thornwood. "No wonder we can never get into their séances. They would not want that information to get out."

"You have not been?" I asked. My heart was sinking. I had been hoping our visitors would be able to tell us all we needed to know about the Loxworths. Clearly, this was not the case.

Harbury shook his head. "No. We have had to study them from afar. We know a great deal about them, except the exact set-up for their séances. They refuse to have anything to do with the Society for Psychical Research."

"Suspicious in and of itself," Holmes commented. "If the phenomena being displayed were genuine, they should have no fear of you studying them."

"Exactly, Mr. Holmes," Harbury said. "There are a few such practitioners that defy explanation, and we have been known to work with them to expose frauds. Then there are others whose own hubris works against them. They believe that their tricks are undetectable."

"And they are not?" I asked.

"Most definitely not," Harbury replied firmly. He turned to my friend. "We may not know how they are doing what they do, but we can tell you about the Loxworths themselves."

Holmes settled back in his seat. "Pray continue, Mr. Harbury."

"The Loxworths are from Wiltshire originally. They came to London approximately two and a half years ago. Their appearance as mediums only came to our attention about a year ago."

"You must understand, Mr Holmes," Reverend Thornwood interjected, "...that there are large numbers of would-be mediums in London and its surroundings, as well as other psychical phenomena that warrant investigation. And not nearly enough members of the society to do everything. The Loxworths were most likely practicing before that, but we did not know about it."

Holmes nodded his understanding.

Harbury continued, "A woman came to us after attending a séance believing them to be frauds that needed to be exposed..."

"Is it possible to contact the woman?" Holmes asked.

"We can certainly try," Harbury replied. "We have her details in our notes."

"Excellent. Pray continue."

"As I have said, the Loxworths would not allow us to attend their meetings. They refuse to have anything to do with anyone from the Society. We have been fobbed off with such tripe as 'our presence would disturb the harmonies.'"

"One doubts just how harmonious such a meeting would be with the Messenger of Death making an appearance," I observed.

Harbury nodded and continued. "We have traced the family back to Wiltshire. They are a man, Edgar, and his three sisters, Eileen, Edith, and Eleanor. Edith and Eleanor are twins. The women are the mediums. They are an attractive family. Dark curly hair, deep brown eyes, and olive complexions. The brother Edgar Loxworth manages them and arranges the séances. To free them from worldly considerations, or so I am told."

"We also believe they may have changed their name with the shift to London," Thornbury added. "We can trace their arrival in London from Wiltshire but cannot trace the family in Wiltshire. Though, to be perfectly honest, we have not had reason to delve deeply into their past."

"Of more interest," Holmes said softly, "…is where they can be found now."

"They live in Bloomsbury," Harbury replied. "On Bedford Way, off Russell Square."

"Interesting choice of location. Bloomsbury is still fairly respectable, but there is a bohemian element as well. We were aware that they lived in Bloomsbury, but not the street," Holmes said. "Thank you for your time, gentlemen, this has been most enlightening."

Taking the hint, our guests rose to leave.

Holmes spoke again. "If you should come across any other information about the Loxworths, I would be obliged if you would let me know."

The men assured him that they would do so, and then took their leave.

Our guests had barely gone, when a knocking at the front door, followed by feminine voices, heralded the arrival of two women.

One of them was Cynthia Taverner. "I apologise for not sending a message around, Mr. Holmes, Dr. Watson, but Mrs. Barthwaite did not wish to wait."

The other lady, Mrs. Barthwaite, nodded somewhat vigorously. "Indeed. I saw no point in sending a message when we could come ourselves."

I saw Cynthia wince at this breech of propriety.

Mrs. Barthwaite was obviously a forthright woman of strong opinions. I took her to be in her early forties. Her hair was blonde and her eyes blue. She gazed strongly out at the world, as if daring it to try to stop her. This was a formidable woman. I was not surprised that she had effectively bullied Cynthia into bringing her to us.

Holmes moved smoothly. "Take a seat ladies and tell us what brings you here."

I hastened to the door, intending to ask Mrs. Hudson for more tea, when I saw the lady coming up the stairs with a fresh tray. I took it from her with a murmur of thanks and placed it on the table. I poured tea for everyone, except Holmes, who was still drinking his coffee, and then settled back in my chair to listen.

It was Cynthia who started. "After your visit, Mr. Holmes, I let a few of my fellow female private enquiry agents know that I had someone who was interested in the Loxworths. Early this afternoon one of them, Nancy Cotterall, brought Mrs. Barthwaite to me. When I heard Mrs. Barthwaite's story, I knew that you needed to know. I was going to send Robert around with a message, but Mrs. Barthwaite had other ideas."

"I was sure, Mr. Holmes, that if you were interested in the Loxworths then it was surely a matter of life or death." The lady paused. "As it was for my sister."

"Your sister?" Holmes asked softly.

"My younger, unmarried sister. Doris Henfold."

Holmes settled back in his chair. "Tell me about your sister, Mrs. Barthwaite."

"Doris and I were the only children of somewhat aged parents. It was agreed that when one of us married, the other would remain to care for our parents. I met and married Mr. Barthwaite. Gerald came down from Nether Poppleton in Yorkshire to find work. He found employment at a bank and rose steadily through the ranks. It was clear that I would not have money worries, so it was agreed with our parents that they should leave everything to Doris."

"Are we talking a large inheritance?" Holmes asked.

"Not particularly, Mr. Holmes," Mrs. Barthwaite replied. "A small house here in Marylebone and enough money that Doris could live comfortably, but not extravagantly." The lady paused and took a sip of her tea. "Our parents died two years ago. It became obvious from the very beginning that Doris felt adrift."

"How long had she cared for your parents?" I asked.

"A little over six years. Mother took ill first, and Doris and father nursed her. Mother died first and father, having lost heart, followed soon afterwards. His heart failed I believe. I contend that he died of a broken heart." The lady gave me a look as if challenging me to disagree with her.

I smiled gently. "I have known of it to happen. People lose a loved one and then die themselves shortly afterwards."

Mrs. Barthwaite gave me a small smile of approval and turned back to Holmes. "Doris did not know what to do with herself. She talked about finding employment. I quashed that idea. Telling her that as she did not need the money, and it was selfish to take a job from someone who did need the money. She saw my point, of course, and began to look around for hobbies to fill her time."

"When did she become involved with the Loxworths?" Cynthia asked.

"I don't rightly know," Mrs. Barthwaite said. "The first I heard of it was when she came to me in great distress."

"What happened?" Holmes asked.

"Early one morning, Doris came racing into my house, upsetting the servants. Thank goodness dear Mr. Barthwaite had already left for work. I sat her down and made her drink some tea. Then it all came blurting out. About the Loxworths, the séances, and the Messenger of Death. Apparently, the night before the Messenger had told Doris she was going to die."

"What did you do?" I asked.

"I suspected a hoax, so I took her to our lawyer. He said there was nothing he could do, except get Doris to draw up a will. Which she did."

"Who is your lawyer?" I asked.

"Mr. Benjamin Cooper of Cooper, Cooper, and Bartholomew in Chancery Lane."

I made a note and nodded for the lady to continue.

"Did your sister mention anything at all to you about other people at the séance or other prophesies of death?" Holmes asked.

Mrs. Barthwaite thought hard. "I remember three names. Steven Smith, Beatrice Oakwood, and Maude Easton. I remember the last one because just before the Messenger said Doris was next to die, they said that Maude Easton had been taken home."

"Three more questions, Mrs. Barthwaite," Holmes said. "What killed your sister, where was she found, and who was the police officer involved?"

Mrs. Barthwaite gave him a sharp look. "It was poison that killed my sister, I do not know what sort. My husband dealt with the police. I found it too distressing and distasteful. However, dear Gerald, whilst an excellent banker, is not the most astute of men. He never thought to ask the policeman investigating the death of poor Doris his name and never thought to ask what poison. It was most unsatisfactory, and I took care to tell him so."

I imagined that she had – at quite some length. I also thought that Mr. Barthwaite was probably more astute than his wife realized. Knowing that she would no doubt harass the poor man, he deliberately 'forgot' his name. As to the poison, to most people one poison is much like another.

Mrs. Barthwaite continued, "As to where Doris was found, she was the room I would least have expected her to be in."

"Pray elucidate," Holmes said softly.

"Our father had a small study not far from the front door. When he died, Doris turned it into a receiving room. Not that she had pretensions above her station, you understand, but so that she had a place to receive people she did not want to let further into the house. I wasn't sure about the idea at first, but when she explained why, I thoroughly approved. One does not want certain people in the heart of one's home after all."

Holmes got to his feet. "Thank you, Mrs. Barthwaite, you have been most helpful. Rest assured that I will do my best to see these villains brought to justice."

"Thank you, Mr. Holmes." Mrs. Barthwaite and Cynthia got to their feet to leave.

"One last thing," Holmes said. "Who did inherit from your sister?"

"My children, Michael and Diana. They are named for my parents. We managed to get Michael into Eton. He will go far with the opportunities Eton affords."

The ladies moved to the door. At the door, Mrs. Barthwaite turned back. "There is one thing, Mr. Holmes. According to Mr. Cooper, when they inventoried Doris's belongings, there was some jewellery missing. I do not know the details. Mr. Cooper originally suspected the maid, but Doris had no live-in staff. Merely a cleaning lady who came in a couple of days a week."

"Interesting," Holmes murmured. "We shall speak with Mr. Cooper for the details."

The ladies took their leave, I escorted them downstairs and into a cab. I took care to let the cabby know that they were acquaintances of Holmes and mine. Holmes had a string of contacts amongst the cabbies of London, much like an adult version of his Baker Street Irregulars.

Chapter Six

When I arose the next morning, Holmes was at the breakfast table before me.

He sat, sipping his coffee with barely concealed impatience, as I tucked in to a plate of bacon, devilled kidneys, and poached eggs.

"When you have finished eating," Holmes said, "I thought we might pay some visits."

I took a sip of my breakfast coffee. It really is a fine, invigorating brew to start the day with. "Whom are we visiting?" I asked.

"I thought we would start with Miss Pappwell. And before you ask, my dear Watson, I sent Wiggins around with both our cards. It would not do to catch the lady unawares."

Wiggins, the leader of the band of street arabs known informally as the Baker Street Irregulars, was a cheeky lad, but one with a heart of gold. I doubted Miss Pappwell would have been too put out when he appeared at her door.

I hastened to finish my breakfast; it appeared

that the game was, once again, afoot.

A cab took us to a small, but stylish, townhouse in Kensington. I admit I was a little surprised at first, but a moment's reflection told me I should not have been. Miss Pappwell had not told us of her background, but that she was her aunt's sole heiress.

Miss Pappwell must have sensed my curiosity. She smiled slightly as she let us in. "This house belonged to my aunt. She rented it out. When I saw it, I knew I wanted to live in it."

"It was certainly better than the house in Islington where we lived before," another female voice added.

I looked up to see another woman walking down the stairs. She was around Miss Pappwell's age, with glossy mahogany coloured hair arranged in a loose chignon. Her morning gown was of a rich green damask linen. She came to Miss Pappwell's side. I noticed her eyes were a vivid shade of green that almost matched her gown.

"Gentlemen," Miss Pappwell said, "…this is Miss Tabitha Reynolds. My companion." She turned to the woman. "Tabby dear, could you please get us some tea?"

"Of course, Kitty," Tabitha replied and headed in the direction of what were, no doubt, the kitchens.

Miss Pappwell led us into a comfortable sitting room that was furnished with several comfortable sofas with rosewood occasional tables close at hand. The walls were dominated by large walnut bookcases that held a vast array of books, both fiction and non-fiction. I was secretly delighted to see a fine, bound copy of *A Study in Scarlet* sitting on one of the shelves.

Miss Reynolds returned, along with a maid pushing a tea-trolley. After we were seated and tea served, Miss Pappwell turned to my friend.

"Have you got news for me, Mr. Holmes?"

"Not yet, I am afraid, Miss Pappwell. I am after information from you."

"Anything I can tell you that will help I will gladly tell you."

"Did your aunt have any live-in staff?"

Miss Pappwell nodded. "Yes, she did. But

Lotty was not working the day my aunt was murdered."

"Do you happen to know the whereabouts of the young lady?" Holmes asked. "I should like to speak with her."

"Did she get another position in London?" I asked, visualising a long traipse around the city looking for the girl.

Miss Pappwell smiled slightly. "She did, and very quickly, too." The smile widened, "I hired her. It was Lotty who brought in the tea just now."

Miss Reynolds got to her feet. "I shall fetch her for you."

Miss Reynolds returned shortly after with the maid in tow. The girl was quite young; I would have put her at no more than sixteen or seventeen years old. She gazed at us shyly, and sat awkwardly on the edge of a chair, twisting the edge of her linen apron in her hands nervously. The girl reminded me of nothing so much as a young doe, ready to flee at the first sight of the hunter.

My friend smiled gently. "Do not be afraid of

us, Miss Lotty, you are not in trouble."

"Sir," the girl whispered.

"I want to ask you about Mrs. Winterbottom. Why you were not there when she died."

The girl looked up at my friend through her lashes. "My sister, Jenny, had just had another baby. Mrs. Winterbottom was real good to work for. She knew I was worried about me sister. Lily, that's me sister, had a bad time o' it when she had her first baby. Mrs. Winterbottom arranged for me to go and stay with me sister to help her."

"Was that unusual for Mrs. Winterbottom?" I asked.

It was Kitty Pappwell that answered. "Not especially, Dr. Watson. My aunt loved children, always regretting that she had been unable to have any of her own. She would always do what she could to help children."

"When did you go to your sister, Miss Lotty?" Holmes asked.

"Three days a'fore it happened. But it was

arranged for me to go mebbee two months a'fore. I got a real shock when Miss Kitty came to tell me. Also real scared, 'cause I was out of a position and me ma needs the money."

"I was aware of Lotty's background," Miss Pappwell said softly. "And I was in need of a maid, so I asked her to work for me."

"Miss Kitty is real good to work for," Lotty said to my friend. "I don't know anything else, mister, I really don't. Can I go back to work now?"

"Of course you can, Miss Lotty," my friend replied.

The girl jumped up from the chair, bobbed a small curtsey, and fairly scurried from the room.

Holmes sat with a small frown on his face. "Had your aunt learned of her impending death by the time Lotty was sent to her sister?"

Miss Pappwell shook her head. "No. It was perhaps two weeks after the decision was made to send Lotty to help her sister that my aunt received that foul prophecy."

Holmes rose to his feet, and I followed. "Thank you for your time, ladies. That was most helpful."

The ladies also rose. "Thank you, Mr. Holmes," Miss Pappwell said. "I know from Dr. Watson's writing that you never explain while the case is ongoing. But when this is over, I would very much like to hear the explanation, if it is not too much trouble."

Holmes inclined his head. "Of course, I shall make sure that you are included. It was, after all, you who set me upon this endeavour."

We took our leave and headed out into the street to get a cab.

I noticed that Holmes was frowning.

"What is wrong, Holmes?"

"I did not wish to say anything in front of Miss Pappwell, but I fear that in sending her maid away, Mrs. Winterbottom signed her own death certificate."

"What on Earth do you mean?"

"If young Lotty had been in the house, then the killer would not have had the opportunity to kill Mrs.

Winterbottom."

"He could have killed the maid as well," I said.

Holmes shook his head. "No. That would have telegraphed to even the thickest of policemen that it was murder. This killer is not interested in the notoriety that follows in murder's wake." My friend shook himself. "Come, Watson, we need to be on our way."

Chapter Seven

A cab was quickly procured, and we were soon on our way to Chancery Lane to visit the Barthwaites' lawyer.

Chancery Lane would have to be one of London's oldest thoroughfares. It was originally known as New Street, having been created by the Knights Templar as a road leading from their old headquarters in Holborn to their new temple. The Temple Church fascinated then as much as it does now. Being a round building with an aura of strangeness surrounding it.

New Street played a dreadful part in the persecution of those of the Jewish faith in the 13th century, when King Henry III founded the *Domus Conversorum*, where Jewish people were held prisoner and instructed in the Christian faith.

What led to the street's name change was Henry III also closing the law schools in the city and setting up the Inns of Chancellery where budding lawyers were apprenticed.

His great-grandson, King Edward III gave the

building that had housed the *Domus Conversorum* to the Keeper of the Rolls of the Court of Chancery. This helped consolidate the legal profession's hold on the street, and it soon became known as Chancery Lane. Chancery being a corruption of chancellery.

Chancery Lane had remained a bastion of lawyers and their associates ever since.

The offices of Cooper, Cooper, and Bartholomew were located about halfway along Chancery Lane, in a fine redbrick Georgian building.

A well-dressed clerk asked our names and our business upon entrance and then hastened away to fetch Mr. Benjamin Cooper.

To my surprise, Benjamin Cooper turned out to be quite a youngish man. I would have taken him to be only a little older than Kitty Pappwell.

When Holmes mentioned Mrs. Barthwaite, he escorted us to his own office.

"I do trust, our clerk, Michael," he said, "…but I really do not like to discuss a client's business in the open."

Holmes nodded his understanding. "An admirable sentiment, Mr. Cooper."

I glanced around the office. It was, perhaps, a trifle tidier than most lawyer's offices I had been in. Book-filled cases lined the walls, with their contents neatly arranged. A brass pen rack on the right side of the desk held several pens: both utilitarian and decorative. Beside it sat a matching inkwell stand containing bottles of black, blue, and red ink. A window behind the desk looked out over Chancery Lane.

Mr. Cooper seated us in two rather comfortable leather upholstered chairs before the desk, before taking his own. "Now gentlemen, perhaps you could tell me what brings Mr. Sherlock Holmes and Dr. John Watson to my office? I will admit to curiosity. I cannot image Gerald Barthwaite being involved in any sort of illegality. He is a man of far too much rectitude to commit a crime."

"It is not Mr. Barthwaite who brings us here, but Mrs. Barthwaite," my friend replied.

Mr. Cooper raised an eyebrow. "Mrs. Barthwaite?"

"To be more precise, that matter of her sister."

The air of gentile levity that Benjamin Cooper wore immediately fell away. "That was a sad and very strange business. Am I to take it that Mrs. Barthwaite has called you in to investigate?"

Holmes shook his head. "No. We are investigating another death, but it is connected."

Cooper leaned forward. "Another death? There was more than poor Miss Henfold's?"

"Likely a great many more," Holmes replied. "But the one we are investigating is that of a Mrs. Amaryllis Winterbottom."

Benjamin Cooper sat back in his seat; his expression thunderstruck. "I knew she was dead. But…"

"You knew Mrs. Winterbottom?" Holmes asked.

"I am a lawyer, Mr. Holmes. As such, I know other lawyers. I deal with them on behalf of clients. I see them around the Inns of Court. I knew Cornelius Winterbottom and had met his wife. Cornelius was a contemporary of my father, the first Cooper of Cooper,

Cooper, and Bartholomew."

"Did you know the Winterbottoms' niece?" I asked.

"Kitty? Oh yes. She is a little younger than I. She was a sweet child, but an absolute terror when roused. My younger brother, Bart, once pulled her pigtails when they were about six. She chased him around the garden with a stick. I doubt that she has changed much."

"The lady is indeed feisty," Holmes agreed. "I understand that there was jewellery missing from Miss Henfold's house after her death?"

"Yes, Mr. Holmes. When I drew up Miss Henfold's will, I inventoried her jewellery. She did not have much, but she had once piece that was really quite good, so it was detailed separately."

"Mrs. Barthwaite says she does not know what it was," Holmes said.

"That would be correct. Mrs. Barthwaite refused to remain in the room when Miss Henfold and I were drawing up the will. She said it would not be decent for her to be present as her children were inheriting the bulk of the estate."

Benjamin Cooper got up and walked to a filing cabinet. "I never saw the piece in question, but it was detailed in the will. When I went to Miss Henfold's house to secure it and do an inventory, as I was also executor of her estate, I could not find that particular item."

"Did Miss Henfold have much jewellery?" I asked.

"She had a small box with a few pieces. Nothing too expensive, but definitely tasteful." He came back to the desk with the will in hand. Unfolding it, he skimmed it quickly, before laying it out on the desk in front of us. I noted he covered as much of the will as he could, allowing us to see only the description.

Holmes read aloud, "...I leave my choker of four strands of pearls with a sardonyx cameo to my niece Diana Barthwaite, to be kept for her by my sister, Daphne Barthwaite until Diana should come of age or marry." He looked up at Cooper. "And you say Mrs. Barthwaite knew nothing of this?"

"Not a thing. She did not even know her sister had such a necklace. Frivolous is how I think she described it."

Personally, I suspected that the late Miss Henfold had not told her sister about her purchase and bequest simply because of her attitude.

Holmes got to his feet, and I followed. "Thank you for your time, Mr. Cooper. It has been most enlightening. May I ask one question, not associated with the case at hand?"

"Of course," Benjamin Cooper asked, his tone now one of amused curiosity.

"Why did your father call the firm Cooper, Cooper, and Bartholomew rather than, say, Cooper and Sons?"

Cooper gave a shout of laughter. "You really are as observant as they say. My father originally had two other partners, but the first one retired when I qualified. When my brother Bart, or, more properly Bartholomew qualified, the other retired. Father felt that Cooper and Sons sounded more like a wine merchant than a firm of lawyers. It was my brother who suggested using his first name."

Benjamin Cooper was still chuckling as he escorted us out. "I hope I have been of assistance, gentlemen."

As we headed out into Chancery Lane I turned to Holmes. "What do we do now?" I asked.

"Now? Now, my friend, we return home and invite Lestrade to supper. It is time to get Scotland Yard involved. We have three murders and no official standing."

I nodded and turned my attention to flagging down a cab.

Mrs. Hudson was pleased to learn that we were inviting Lestrade to supper. Our landlady was firmly convinced that the good inspector did not eat properly, so was quite happy to feed him whenever the opportunity arose.

Lestrade, who mostly existed on meat pies from a pie shop near his lodgings, was quite happy to dine with us whenever the invitation was extended. So, it was a very happy man who arrived at our door just before seven o'clock that night.

Mrs. Hudson excelled herself. She presented us with a fine meal of oyster soup, followed by baked haddock with boiled artichokes, and stewed cucumbers with onions. This was followed by baked carrot pudding with cream. The pudding did not sound terribly appetising, but it was truly delicious, combining carrots with breadcrumbs, suet, eggs, milk, raisins, currents, sugar, and nutmeg. We dined in companionable silence, until Lestrade dabbed at his lips with his napkin, and pushed his chair back from the table.

He smiled at Mrs. Hudson when she came to clear the table. "That was an excellent repast. Thank you."

"You are most welcome, Inspector. Now, will you gentlemen be wanting tea or coffee?"

"No thank you, Mrs. Hudson," Holmes said. "I think brandy is called for."

Mrs. Hudson nodded her agreement and swiftly cleared the table, leaving us alone to talk. I poured brandy for us all and we settled into the comfortable chairs around the fireplace. It was a chilly night, and I was thankful that Mrs. Hudson had lit the fire sometime earlier that evening.

Lestrade took a sip of his brandy. "Now gentlemen, what favour do you need that leads you to invite me to supper?"

"Could we not just want the pleasure of your company?" I asked, matching Lestrade's lightly amused tone with one of my own.

"You could. But it is highly unlikely."

"We have a new case," Holmes said softly. "And it involves murder."

Lestrade's levity fell away, and he leaned towards my friend. "Tell me about it."

Lestrade listened carefully as Holmes related what Kitty Pappwell and, later, Daphne Barthwaite had told us about the dreadful deaths and the missing jewellery.

"I don't suppose it is suicide?" Lestrade asked.

The look Holmes gave him was scathing. "What did they do, Lestrade? Drink the poison then go to the scullery and wash the cup and put it away?"

I decided to add my piece, "Besides, the poison used on Mrs. Winterbottom was black henbane, which causes death by respiratory paralysis. Anyone who drank a sufficient quantity of it would not be able to walk from the scullery to the places they were found. They would most likely have been found in ungainly heaps upon the floor."

Lestrade raised his hands in a gesture of surrender. "You cannot blame me for hoping, gentlemen. If I take the tale of the Messenger of Death to my superiors, they will most likely recommend a nice long stay for me in Colney Hatch or a similar establishment."

"We are not dealing with a supernatural killer, Lestrade. This is a very cunning, very avaricious, murderer. And I can guarantee that he is flesh and blood, not some sort of ghastly ghoul."

"I do not know much about such things," I said, "…but you might want to point out that something already dead would have no use for jewellery."

Lestrade sighed. "You are both correct." He got out his notebook and wrote down the names of Amaryllis Winterbottom, Doris Henfold, and Maude

Easton. "I shall see what information I can find on the investigations. I warn you; I doubt it will be much. If they were written off as suicides, then the bare minimum effort will have been expended."

Holmes nodded. "Understandable. Any information you can acquire will be useful, Lestrade."

Holmes also gave him the names of the two other attendees that Doris Henfold had mentioned to her sister: Steven Smith and Beatrice Oakwood, and of course, the Loxworth family.

Lestrade finally snapped his notebook shut and tucked it into his waistcoat pocket. Getting to his feet, he said, "Well, if we cannot convict them of murder, we will at least be able to get them under the Witchcraft Act of 1735."

The Witchcraft Act of 1735 was actually quite a humane law, compared to the previous ones, that saw the transfer of the prosecution of alleged witches from the ecclesiastical courts to the secular ones. The law forbade anyone to claim to have any sort of magical powers or abilities. Unlike the previous witchcraft laws, the penalties were fines and imprisonment, not death.

Wishing us both a goodnight, Lestrade left our rooms. We heard him call out a goodnight to Mrs. Hudson as he left the building.

Chapter Eight

The following morning saw a surprise in the form of a message from Langdale Pike asking us to visit him at his club that morning.

Langdale Pike spent all of his waking hours ensconced in the bow window of his club. Usually, he gave the appearance of ignoring the passing parade of people. That morning, however, it was clear that he had been watching and waiting for us.

Pike rose to his feet even before the club's footman had escorted us to his table.

Coffee was served by the same footman before Pike waved him away.

"Thank you for coming, Sherlock."

"I admit to being intrigued," Holmes replied. "It is rare for you to send a message asking for our attendance. You have found something?"

"I have." Pike paused. "I have found another victim."

I stared at him, aghast. "Another victim of the Loxworths?"

Pike nodded. "I asked discreetly around the club."

"Asked the members?" I asked.

"Not just the members," Holmes said softly. "You would never overlook such a valuable source as the staff, would you, Langdale?"

Pike smiled briefly. "Of course not. I get some of my most valuable information from servants."

"A servant was a victim?" I asked.

Pike shook his head. "The victim I found was a lady named Harriet Abercrombie. She was from a reasonably well-to-do family but was left in straightened circumstances on the death of her husband. Her son works here as a footman. I have told him only that you are investigating the Loxworths. He is keen to speak with you."

Holmes got to his feet. "Send him to our rooms when he is free. He will be available this evening?"

"He will and I shall do so," Pike replied.

"Come, Watson," Holmes said.

"Are we going back home?" I asked, as we exited the club.

Holmes shook his head. "No. I think a visit to Scotland Yard is called for. Lestrade needs to add another victim to his list."

A short cab ride took us to Scotland Yard. When Holmes asked for Lestrade and said who he was, the response, at least from the rank and file, was almost idolatrous.

I smiled to myself, thinking of the early days, when Holmes was not particularly liked by Scotland Yard and most definitely not welcome.

Over the years, I had seen the changes, as the detectives realised that Holmes was no amateur playing at detective, but a man of genuine insight and intellect, who had something to offer them. It also helped that Holmes preferred to allow the credit for solving cases to go to the inspector in charge.

Several of the inspectors, like Lestrade, and MacDonald, whom Holmes referred to as 'friend MacDonald' and 'Mr. Mac,' had become genuine friends.

We were quickly shown to Lestrade's office. The man looked up as we were announced by an excited constable.

"I hope you haven't come looking for results. I have not had time to even start yet."

"We have come to add to your list," Holmes said, taking one of the chairs in front of Lestrade's desk and gesturing for me to take the other.

Lestrade sat up straighter. "Another name?"

"We were informed this morning of the name of another victim. Her son will be visiting Baker Street this evening. We thought you might like to be present," Holmes said.

"I would," Lestrade agreed. "What time do you want me there?" His expression was vaguely hopeful. Even I could tell he was hoping for more of Mrs. Hudson's food.

Holmes gave a small half-smile. "I doubt we will see our visitor before eight o'clock. Come at seven, Lestrade, and dine with us again."

Lestrade was profuse in his thanks, and we left

him humming happily to himself.

Back out on the street, Holmes turned to me, his tone one of light good humour. "Policemen are rather like stray dogs, don't you think, Watson?"

"Whatever do you mean, Holmes?"

"Feed them once, and you are always feeding them."

He turned away with a smile to hail a cab, as I guffawed with laughter.

Supper that evening was a much more subdued affair than that of the previous night. Though Mrs. Hudson had again provided a feast of barley soup, followed by fish and oyster pie with cabbage and marrow, followed by damson pudding with cream. We ate quietly and quickly as we waited for our visitor.

The footman from Langdale Pike's club arrived a little after eight o'clock. He gave his name as Albert Abercrombie.

"Mr. Pike told me to come and see you gentlemen. He said you were investigating other people who died after visiting the Loxworths."

"We are, Mr. Abercrombie," Holmes said. Please, take a seat and tell us what happened to your mother."

Abercrombie, who was tall and well-built, carefully lowered himself into one of our chairs by the fire. I hastened to get him a brandy. I thought he might need one to help him relax and tell us his story. After a moment's thought, I poured brandies for Holmes, Lestrade, and myself as well.

"My father died three years ago. He left us with the house, but very little money. Turned out he was a gambler. Thankfully he hadn't got much into debt, but mother had to let all, but one, of the servants go, and let out rooms. A friend of my father's got me the job at the club."

"Do you like working there?" I asked.

Abercrombie shrugged. "They pay well, and the work is easy. The gentlemen are mostly polite and easy to look after. It could have been a lot worse."

I nodded. Abercrombie was correct. For a man of his background, who no doubt grew up expecting to be one of the leisured classes, finding and keeping any sort of a position could be difficult. Certainly, working as a footman, or usher, at a prestigious club was better pay and working conditions than working as a footman for some aristocratic family where he would be little better than a male maid, shifting heavy furniture for the maids to clean and other such jobs.

"The lodgers were mostly young professional men, who paid reasonably well for their room and two meals a day. After a while, mother was able to start saving a little money. Then someone, I do not know who, told her about the Loxworths." Abercrombie paused and took a sip of his brandy. "Mother had never forgiven father for gambling away his money. I think she wanted to talk with him from beyond the grave simply to give him a piece of her mind."

I smiled briefly at the image of a woman hectoring the dead via a medium. I did not know much about mediums, but I was sure that was not a situation that they normally encountered.

"Did she tell you about the Messenger of Death?" Holmes asked softly.

"She did," Abercrombie replied. "I told her it was a lot of nonsense and to stop going. She agreed with me and said that was her last attendance."

"What happened on the day your mother died?" Lestrade asked. I noticed that he had his notebook out and was writing down Albert Abercrombie's story.

"On the day that she was told she was going to die, I asked her to go and stay with her sister for the day. You see, gentlemen, with the lodgers being professionals, there was rarely anyone at home during the day."

"What about the maid?" Holmes asked.

"Sylvia doesn't live in. She came in during the morning and helped mother clean up after breakfast and clean the lodger's rooms. Then she and mother would have a light lunch. After that they would clean the living room, parlour, and our private rooms, and get everything ready for mother to cook the evening meal. It was usually around four o'clock when Sylvia left. The first of the lodgers wouldn't get in until around six-thirty."

"This was the routine every day?" Holmes asked.

"It was, Mr. Holmes. I had a room at home, but

I live-in at the club. Room and board are included in my wages. It meant that I could give most of my money to my mother."

"Who found your mother?" Lestrade asked.

"Jeremy Greene. He is a banker's clerk in the City. He told me that he got in at six-thirty-five. He said he knew something was wrong the moment he walked in. My mother was always there to greet her boys, as she called them. She wasn't there, so Jeremy went looking. He found her seated in the front parlour. Dead. That was when Simon Radcliffe returned home. Simon is a junior barrister. He sent for the police and for me."

"The police said it was suicide. That mother was depressed following the death of my father. She was when he died, but by that point she had found a new reason for living in her lodgers and her new life as a landlady. Mother was enjoying life. She would not have ended it."

"We tend to agree, Mr. Abercrombie," Holmes said. "Your mother was a victim of murder. One of four by our reckoning."

"And there are probably more," I added.

Albert Abercrombie stared at us, aghast. "I hope you find the monster, gentlemen. If I can help in any way, please, send for me."

"We shall do so," Holmes assured him. "There is one more thing."

"Mr. Holmes?"

"Were any of your mother's possessions missing after her death?"

"Yes. When I went through her jewellery, looking for a keepsake for Sylvia, I noticed that her gold locket was missing. It was an oval shape about the size of a sovereign and engraved with my mother's initials, which were HEA, she was Harriet Emily Abercrombie, surrounded by roses. My father had given it to her on their first wedding anniversary."

Holmes got to his feet. "Thank you, Mr. Abercrombie. You have been most helpful."

"Thank you, Mr. Holmes." Albert Abercrombie nodded to us and took his leave.

After Mr. Abercrombie left, Holmes sat for a

while, frowning to himself.

Lestrade and I exchanged looks. "What is our next move, Holmes?" I finally asked.

"We need to know how the Loxworths are getting their information. The killer is only killing people who are alone. Even if there is a live-in maid, they are, most conveniently not there when the deaths occur. No-one has mentioned any untoward visitors seeking information."

"The families may not know," I said. "After all, does Mrs. Hudson mention every hawker who comes to her door during the day?"

"An excellent point, my dear Watson! We will make a detective out of you yet."

"What do you plan to do?" Lestrade asked.

"We shall call in the experts, Lestrade. If anyone knows how the Loxworths are coming by this information, it will be Major Donald Porthey, Reverend Andrew Thornwood, and the 'Amazing' Jonathan Harbury."

Holmes sent a message to Major Porthey early

the next morning. A message was received back inviting us to Major Porthey's home that afternoon.

Lestrade was informed and he joined us at Baker Street just after lunch.

Major Porthey lived in a fine modern townhouse in Fitzhardinge Street in Marylebone, not too far from Baker Street. As the day was still pleasant, we elected to walk there.

Major Porthey greeted us pleasantly and led us into what was clearly a library. There were cases of books of obvious interest to someone involved in psychical research, but also books on archaeology, history, religion, and the sciences, as well as a scattering of fiction, poetry, and plays.

Andrew Thornwood and Jonathan Harbury were already seated waiting for us. Lestrade was introduced and there was a pause as we settled in comfortably and tea was fetched.

Porthey picked up his cup and turned towards my friend. "Your message said that you had a question for us?"

Holmes nodded. "I do. The question is this: how would a fraudulent medium set about getting information about a person?"

Harbury leaned back in his seat. "There are a number of ways to go about it, depending on the location. In smaller towns, for example, one trick is to send someone into the town a few months before the medium's visit. They wander around the town, noting the businesses and who owns them. Another thing they do is visit the local cemeteries."

"Cemeteries?" I asked, slightly puzzled.

"Of course!" Holmes exclaimed. "Cemeteries would be excellent sources of local information. So much is inscribed on headstones."

Harbury nodded. "Dates of birth and death, spouse, children. Often parents and siblings as well. Quite often these days the cause of death is added too."

Andrew Thornwood spoke up, "The local parish churches with their records are also a good source. As is listening to the talk in shops, tearooms, and bars."

Porthey joined in. "The confederate writes down all the information and takes it back to the medium. A month or two later, the medium rolls into town. They advertise that they are doing a small number of sittings. It is always the most prominent people who attend first, and those are the people it is easiest to find facts about. After the first séance where the mayor's great-aunt Mavis who died of cholera in 1858 makes an 'appearance' everyone who is anyone comes flocking."

Harbury nodded. "The medium does a very small number of sittings. Most likely no more than six or seven. And then moves on to another town."

Holmes nodded his understanding. "A town that the confederate has already visited and obtained as much relevant information as they could."

"Exactly," Porthey said.

Harbury spoke again, "There are claims that there are documents known as *Blue Books* in which that information is compiled and circulated around the various mediums. That they are continually being updated."

Thornwood shook his head. "There is no evidence for the existence of those books at all. It is a bit like the Holy Grail to some investigators," he explained to us. "If they can prove the existence of the *Blue Books* then they can prove all mediums are frauds. Some investigators are not much better than the mediums that they investigate."

"Like anything else, Andrew," Harbury said, "...motive is everything. Not everyone in the S.P.R. has good motives for being there."

Thornwood sighed his agreement but said nothing else.

"That system, however well it works in smaller towns, does not work in big cities where the population tends to be more mobile," Harbury said. "In the cities I am told that the medium's sources tend to be people who work in hotels, in trains, in brothels, or domestics in wealthy households."

I found myself thinking of both Langdale Pike and Mycroft Holmes, both of whom surely had informants in all those places, but for entirely different reasons.

Harbury paused, "Believe to be, I should say. I personally do not believe it is possible to sustain it without a huge outlay of money and people who will keep quiet without blackmailing you. I never worked as a medium, but part of my stage act included 'knowing' all sorts of facts about members of my audience. It was an awful lot of work just getting the information, and frankly, not worth the time and the effort. I soon moved on to illusions and magic tricks."

"Interesting," Holmes murmured, "…and not unlike how I myself have been known to work."

"I am trying to contact the woman who brought the Loxworths to our attention," Harbury said. "But I have not had any success as yet. I shall keep trying."

"Thank you, Mr. Harbury," Holmes said. "It is much appreciated."

"There is another way," Harbury said. "It tends to be used when the fraud has a particular mark in mind."

"What is that?" I asked.

"They send people to ask around the neighbourhood. Nothing suspicious that would make someone tell the person. Posing as someone selling things at the door. A knife grinder perhaps, or selling spoons, or even a ginger beer vendor. It is simplicity itself to get the servants to talk. Do they know anyone else who would be interested. What about that nice, big, house on the corner?"

Holmes looked thoughtful.

"Is there anything else you need from us?" Major Porthey asked.

Holmes nodded. "I believe there is. I have heard from family members of Loxworth sitters, I am hoping to hear from people who have attended the séances, and from those investigating the Loxworths. There is one point of view that I am missing."

"And what is that?" Reverend Thornwood asked.

"The point of view of another medium. I should very much like to speak with a reputable medium on the subject. If anyone would know such a person, if would be you gentlemen."

Porthey shook his head. "There I personally cannot help. I believe I mentioned to you at our first meeting that hauntings of places are my area of interest."

"I am sure that Jonathan and I can arrange someone," Reverend Thornwood added.

Harbury nodded. "It may take us a while, however. Very few mediums, whether fraudulent or not, will be happy be help when they hear that Scotland Yard is involved." He looked pointedly at Lestrade.

Lestrade shrugged. "We are investigating several cases of probable murder. I don't really care if we get help from someone who claims to be in touch with the Archangel Gabriel, so long as the information is good."

All three of the gentlemen chuckled gently at Lestrade's sally.

Porthey got to his feet. Everyone else followed suit. Porthey escorted us to the front door. "We will be in touch as soon as we find someone willing to help."

He shook our hands once again, and we left.

Outside, evening was setting in, and it was becoming gloomy. We hailed cabs and went our separate ways; Lestrade to Scotland Yard, and Holmes and I to Baker Street.

It was almost full-dark by the time we reached home, though it was only around six o'clock, the darkness and the chill in the air told us that winter was rapidly approaching.

My friend had an air of abstraction about him, that told me he was deep in thought about the case. We ate the supper Mrs. Hudson had provided in silence.

After we had eaten, Holmes went and dragged out his scrapbooks of crime, and I noticed, a gazetteer of Wiltshire. Seeing that Holmes was likely to be occupied for the rest of the evening, I took my book, William Morris's interesting utopian novel, *News from Nowhere*, and retired to my room. I suspected that Holmes was unlikely to sleep much that night.

Chapter Nine

I was proved correct, for when I emerged from my room the next morning, Holmes was still in the sitting room, and still wearing the previous day's clothes. He was curled up in his chair reading the Wiltshire gazetteer.

"Good morning," I said cheerfully, as Mrs. Hudson entered bearing plates of sausage, eggs, and bacon. She returned my greeting before hastening out, only to return with a platter of hot toast and a pat of butter, as well as the coffee pot.

At the smell of coffee, Holmes looked up from his reading. He got to his feet, yawned, and then stretched, and joined me at the breakfast table.

I waited for a few minutes, until Holmes had drunk some coffee and had a few mouthfuls of food.

"Did you find anything interesting?" I asked.

Holmes nodded. "I believe I have found the general area in Wiltshire that the Loxworth family comes from. If necessary Lestrade can contact the Wiltshire Constabulary."

"Good God, Holmes!" I exclaimed. "How on Earth did you find that?"

My friend chuckled. "Simplicity itself, my friend. Last names are very evocative of the past. Your name, for example, means 'son of Wat.' Wat was the medieval abbreviation of Walter. Somewhere in your remote past you had an ancestor named Walter who had a son who was known as, shall we say, John Wat's son."

"I had never really thought about the origin of my family name. I do know that names like Cooper and Fletcher derive from occupations."

Holmes nodded. "Barrel-maker and arrow-maker respectively."

"What does Holmes mean?" I asked, suddenly curious.

"It has several meanings," my friend replied. "Mostly because there are similar words in the older English dialects and the language of the northmen known as Vikings. The word 'holm' can mean holly tree or a small island. So, I had an ancestor who either lived near a holly tree or on an island."

"And Loxworth?" I asked.

"I found a Loxworth Manor in the gazetteer," Holmes replied. "It is a medieval ruin not far from the village of Compton Chamberlayne."

"So, the family is from that village?"

"Perhaps, and perhaps not. If it is their family name, then we can safely say that some ancestor was associated with Loxworth Hall. Or they may simply have chosen Loxworth as an alias when they began."

"Either way," I said. "It is an unusual name, so they must have known of the existence, at least, of Loxworth Manor. Very few people read gazetteers for entertainment."

Holmes gave me a wry smile and returned to his breakfast. He finished eating, got to his feet, and headed to his bedroom for a change of clothes and a little sleep.

I helped Mrs. Hudson clear the table and then took myself to Regent's Park for a brisk morning walk.

I had been back for perhaps half an hour and was entertaining myself reading the morning newspapers, when Lestrade arrived. His expression was glum.

I carefully folded the copy of the *Morning Post* that I had been reading and placed it on the arm of Holmes's chair for him to peruse later.

I then went and roused Holmes from his bed. My friend had obviously heard Lestrade's arrival, because he was getting dressed as I poked my head around the door.

When I returned to the living room, Lestrade was settled in his usual chair. He sat in silence until Holmes joined us.

"I take it that you do not have good news for us," Holmes observed.

Lestrade sighed. "I have discovered not one, but three, instances of incompetence by my colleagues in connection with this case. Forgive me for feeling a little unhappy about it."

"Three?" I asked.

"Two more possible murders. Men this time. Both poisoned, both lived alone, and there was no sign of the method of administration of the poison found.

Both cases fell under the jurisdiction of Inspector Miles Lovell. While Lovell is not a stupid man, I do think that *three* similar poisoning cases might have registered as more than a little unusual." Lestrade's features set into a sour expression. "The third one is that I have found Steven Smith."

"Steven Smith?" I asked, momentarily forgetting where I had heard the name.

"One of the attendees that Mrs. Barthwaite mentioned," Holmes said, a trifle brusquely.

"Surely that is good news?" I said, a note of query in my voice.

Lestrade sighed again. "It would be. Except that he came to Scotland Yard to report the Loxworths as fraudulent as described in the Witchcraft Act of 1735. The sergeant on the counter took down the details and then promptly forgot about it. This was two months ago! It wasn't until word went round the Yard that I was looking into the Loxworth family, that he came to me, somewhat shamefacedly, with his notebook."

"Is Mr. Smith's address in these notes?" Holmes

asked.

"It is," Lestrade replied.

"Excellent," Holmes said. He made his way to our coat stand and collected his coat and a hat. "Come gentlemen, time to be on our way."

I got to my feet, and Lestrade followed. "Where are we going?" I asked.

"To see what Inspector Lovell has to say for himself, and then to see Mr. Smith, who I am sure will be delighted that the police are finally taking an interest in his complaint."

Lestrade winced perceptibly but did not comment.

"Come, gentlemen," Holmes said again, and headed out of the door.

Lestrade and I followed swiftly behind him.

Chapter Ten

Inspector Lovell was based at E Division, which was headquartered in the Grays Inn Road Police Station which was, confusingly, actually situated at 70 Theobalds Road in Holborn.

Miles Lovell was an older man. Maybe ten years older than Lestrade. His dark hair was gray at the temples, lending him a distinguished air. That was the only distinguished thing about him. The man had faded blue eyes that held a mixture of anger and petulance. This was a bitter man who had never made it to the heights he thought he deserved and was now doing the bare minimum necessary to keep his job. I had seen it before. It is not good in any industry, but in something like a police officer, could be utterly disastrous.

Lestrade recognised it immediately. I could see the little man's hackles rise. Lestrade was proud to be a police officer and had no time at all for men like Miles Lovell.

Lovell was offhand with us. Refusing even to countenance that they could be murders. "They were suicides. I told that silly little chit that her precious aunty killed herself. Of course she did. So did the two men. You people just go looking for murder."

Lestrade stepped right into the taller man's space. When he spoke, his voice was cold and even. "When certain points were raised about the cases in question, my superiors, and your superiors both agreed that there is reasonable cause to doubt your insistence on suicide. So much so that Scotland Yard is now taking over…"

"Typical," Lovell sneered. "You lot at A Division think you can swan in, push good men out of the way, while bringing in your poncy amateurs." He levelled a look of loathing at Holmes and myself.

"I would stop right there, if I were you," Lestrade said coldly. "Your incompetence is obvious to anyone within the force. We would like to keep it that way. The public does not need to know that there are men like you in the force. If you don't want to finish your career outside of the Metropolitan Police shepherding ducklings across the road in Piddlehinton, then I suggest you change your attitude."

Lovell glared down at him, but Lestrade did not flinch. He returned Lovell's bitter, hateful, stare with a cold, determined one of his own. Eventually, Lovell backed down, turning his head away.

"I have read your reports," Lestrade said. "Have you anything to add to them?"

Lovell shook his head. "Nothing."

"Nothing?" Holmes queried. "You did not leave out, for instance, anything that did not fit your suicide theory?"

Lovell mustered up a half-hearted glare. "I put in all the evidence there was. The men and the woman were dead by poison. That is it!"

Holmes gave the inspector a disgusted look and turned towards the door. "Come, Lestrade, we are wasting our time here."

Lestrade nodded and walked away from his colleague. At the door he stopped and turned back. "You might want to think about your future, Lovell. I will be suggesting a change of posting for you."

"Dorset can be very pleasant in the summer," Holmes added, "…but less so in the winter."

"Dorset?" Lovell looked bewildered.

"Piddlehinton is in Dorset," Lestrade said flatly as we left.

As the door to Lovell's office closed, we could hear the man start to swear.

Out on the street, Lestrade was sunk in gloomy silence as Holmes looked for a cab.

"Cheer up, Lestrade," I said. "It really was too much to hope for that Inspector Lovell would be helpful."

"Indeed," Holmes added, as a cab drew up at his signal. "Let us hope that Mr. Smith is more inclined to be of assistance."

The address that Lestrade had was for a smart shop in fashionable Knightsbridge, not far from the extremely affluent department store, Harrods, which had been opened in 1849 by Charles Henry Harrod to capitalise on the influx of people expected to attend the Great Exhibition which was to be staged in 1851 in nearby Hyde Park. The store, which carried only goods of the finest quality, was a success from the start. The building burned down in 1883 but was swiftly rebuilt. The presence of this remarkable shop, which was popular with the rich and famous, including members of the Royal Family, had made this area of Knightsbridge both fashionable and somewhat exclusive.

Mr. Steven Smith operated a little store selling gentleman's accessories. It exuded an air of quiet good taste and understated elegance, as did its owner.

Mr. Smith was well-dressed and affable. When he heard the reason for our visit, he gestured to his shop clerk to take over the counter and ushered us out the back.

The room we were taken to was dominated by a smallish, well-polished, walnut table with matching chairs. A small stove, just large enough to boil a kettle on, or perhaps an egg or two, sat in the corner. Mr. Smith sat us down and hastened to make tea. A narrow two door cabinet to the right of the stove held cups, saucers, and similar crockery. A small cupboard set onto the wall to the left of the stove revealed a small store of tea, sugar, and biscuits. Fresh milk in a covered jug already sat upon the table. The tea was from Harrods and the biscuits were from Fortnum and Mason. It was obvious that Mr. Smith liked the good things of life and could afford to indulge in them.

When we were all supplied with tea, Mr. Smith selected a crisp ginger biscuit from the tin and looked at us across the table. "I was beginning to despair of anyone at Scotland Yard taking any notice of my complaint."

Lestrade smiled grimly. "As soon as I was made aware of your complaint, I responded."

Smith gave him a shrewd look. "Only learned about it today?"

"Something like that," Lestrade replied.

"The sergeant I spoke to did not seem particularly interested in my compliant."

"The sergeant you spoke to his learned the error of his ways," Lestrade said.

Smith smiled softly. "I am sure he has. Did he tell you exactly what I told him?"

"He said that you wished to report the Loxworth mediums as fraudulent under the Witchcraft Act of 1735."

"I did," Smith acknowledged. "…but, Inspector Lestrade, I also told him that I suspected them of murder."

"Did you now?" Holmes murmured softly.

"Yes, Mr. Holmes. I may not be a detective, but I am a rational and, I like to think, intelligent man. It made no sense to me that any being could predict death so constantly and with such success without the hand of some devil in human form being involved."

Lestrade took out his notebook. "I believe you were present when the announcement was made that Maude Easton had died?"

"I was. That was when I decided that, even though it was only my third séance and I had paid for six, I would not be going back. Walking out afterwards, someone, I do not know his name, the Loxworths did not introduce sitters to each other, mentioned that it was the second death that he was personally aware of."

"If the Loxworths did not introduce their sitters, how did anyone know anyone else's name?" I asked.

Smith shrugged. "People introduced themselves

if they were interested. And the Loxworths did mention people by name during the sittings. It wasn't too hard to work out who each person was. If you were interested enough."

"And you were not interested?" Holmes asked.

"Not especially," Smith replied. "I am more of an observer than a joiner. I went along because I was curious, nothing more."

Lestrade was still making notes. "Did the man you spoke to say whom the victim the other death he was aware of was?"

Smith thought for a moment. "It was another woman. A flower name, and an unusual one at that. Amaryllis. That's it. Amaryllis."

"Did the Loxworths predict another death while you were there?" I asked.

Smith shook his head. "No. Maude Easton's was prophesied on my first visit. Her death announced on my third. That was enough for me." He looked at us sombrely across the table. "There has been another death, hasn't there?"

Holmes nodded. "One, at least, that we know of. Miss Doris Henfold."

Smith looked thoughtful. "I believe I met the lady. A calm, rational, sort of woman. I formed the opinion that she was there for much the same reason I was. Sheer curiosity. No deeply held beliefs about life after death, just a very natural curiosity about the world about her. It seemed to me that if the dead came through, all well and good, but if they didn't, well, it was still a more interesting way to spend an evening instead of sitting at home at knitting or tatting or something along those lines."

It was clear that Mr. Smith did not have any more information for us, so we took our leave.

Outside the shop I commented, "Mr. Smith made Miss Henfold sound like a completely different person than the one her sister described."

Holmes snorted in amusement. "Siblings always see each other in a different light from other people. Your description of me, for example, and Mycroft's, would make anyone think two totally different men were being described."

I thought for a moment, then nodded my agreement. Having had a brother myself, I understood what Holmes meant.

Lestrade sighed. "That visit really did not help very much, did it?"

"On the contrary, Lestrade," Holmes replied. "We are gathering information. A picture of the Loxworths, and the situation, is beginning to form, and it is not a pretty one."

"Murder is never pretty," Lestrade said glumly.

On that pronouncement we hailed a cab and left Knightsbridge for our own part of London.

Lestrade took the cab back to Scotland Yard after Holmes and I alighted at Baker Street.

Chapter Eleven

Holmes spent the rest of the day poring through his scrapbooks of crime looking for any link at all to Wiltshire in general and Loxworth Manor in particular. As his temper became more and more uncertain, I took myself out for another brisk walk. Two walks in one day was certainly not the norm for me, but I felt that, under the circumstances, removing myself from the premises for a short while was a good idea.

On my way back to the flat, I purchased the afternoon papers. When I returned, Holmes had sunk into a gloom, smoking a pipe and staring out of the window.

I sorted out the papers, leaving some in reach of Holmes, then settled in to read *The Daily Telegraph*. As is my wont, I went first to the obituary pages. Not so much to see if anyone I knew had died, but in case there was something that might be of interest to Holmes.

As I scanned down the list of names I froze. "Holmes," I said softly.

I received a grunt in reply.

"The lady that Mrs. Barthwaite mentioned. It was Beatrice Oakwood, was it not?"

"It was."

"I see. It is just that there is a Miss Beatrice Oakwood here in the obituaries."

Holmes leaped to his feet and snatched the paper from my hand. He scanned it swiftly, then threw it down upon the chair.

"Quickly, my good Watson. Get your coat. We must get Lestrade and visit the Oakwoods."

I donned my coat and hat, then picked up the newspaper, folded it carefully, and put it in my coat pocket. We would need to show it to Lestrade.

Scotland Yard was buzzing like a kicked over beehive when we arrived. Not an uncommon state being, as it was, the heart of the London Metropolitan Police.

An earnest young constable escorted us to Lestrade's little office. The man himself was seated at his desk going through some papers. He looked up with some surprise when the constable announced us.

"I only saw you gentlemen a matter of hours ago. What brings you here? Has there been a development in the case?"

"There has," I said. I withdrew the newspaper from my pocket and laid it on Lestrade's desk in front of him. His quick eyes fell, almost immediately, on the name Beatrice Oakwood. He drew in a sharp breath and then swore. "Another one!"

"Another one," Holmes agreed. "But this time we are much closer to the case. You note the date of death was only yesterday?'

Lestrade read the obituary again and then nodded. "So it is."

"Come then," Holmes said. "Let us pay a visit to the address listed and pay our respects."

The newspaper listed an address in Chelsea. Lestrade arranged for a police brougham for us, and we set off.

The address given in the obituary was a tidy townhouse tucked away on Christchurch Terrace. A quiet street quite removed from the hustle of fashionable Chelsea.

Chelsea had long been a favourite place for the great and the good to dwell. Starting from the time of King Henry VIII when Sir Thomas More and Anne of Cleves both dwelt in Chelsea. Dante Gabriel Rossetti, Mary Shelley, Algernon Charles Swinburne, and Oscar Wilde had all called Chelsea home at some point in their lives.

A tall, slender, young man, with dark blonde hair, deep blue eyes, and a nervous disposition opened the door to our knock. When he learned who we were he started to babble. "It was an accident. My aunt would never take her own life. She…"

Lestrade held up a hand in a shushing gesture. "We are not here about a suicide. In fact, I think we can quite categorically state that your aunt did not, in fact, commit suicide."

Suicide, or self-murder, was considered a crime at that time. Such a tag attached to the death could lead to much misery for surviving family members.

The startled young man blinked at us for a few

moments, and then stepped back and gestured for us to enter.

"My apologies, gentlemen. I have been most distraught by my aunt's death. Not to mention the attitude of the local vicar who does not want to give my aunt a Christian burial, because she, in his words, 'performed an un-Christian act.'"

"Is the vicar here?" Lestrade asked softly.

The young man shook his head.

Lestrade walked to the door and went out. He called up to the constable who had driven the brougham. "Nip around to the local church, lad, and bring the vicar here. I don't care what he says. Bring him here. Even if you have to clap the darbies on him."

The constable grinned, and having ascertained the location of the church from our uncertain host, hastened off on his errand. Obviously delighted at the possibility of putting handcuffs on a clergyman.

Lestrade turned back. "If you don't mind, sir, I would like to wait until the vicar is here before we continue. It is not a tale that I want to tell twice."

Our bemused host led us back inside. "Forgive me my lack of manners, gentlemen. My name is Hubert Oakwood. Beatrice Oakwood was my father's youngest sister."

"I take it the lady never married," I said.

Oakwood nodded. "She remained unmarried to care for my grandparents. In his will, my grandfather left this house to my father with the proviso that my Aunt Beatrice be allowed to live the rest of her life here." He pulled a face. "My grandfather was a little old-fashioned about leaving property to women. A ridiculous notion. My mother has as astute a brain as my father."

"It is, unfortunately, not an uncommon opinion," Holmes said.

Hubert Oakwood nodded sadly.

Conversation lagged until the return of the constable accompanied by, not one, but two clergymen.

The first gentleman of the cloth was a drooping individual with the demeanour of a whipped cur. I wondered at what the constable had said to him. Until I took a good look at the second man.

"Reverend Thornwood," Holmes said with a slight smile. "A pleasure to see you again. I take it that you and my good Watson share a hobby of reading the obituary columns in the papers."

Thornwood returned the smile. "I have been continuing my research into the Loxworths and had come across Miss Oakwood's name. When I saw the obituary, I paid a call on the Reverend Little here." His voice hardened. "We were having a nice little chat on Christian charity when the constable arrived."

The way the Reverend Little cringed told me that the chat on Christian charity had been about his own lack of it. "I understand from my colleague here that things have changed?" His voice had a distinct whine to it.

"No sir," Lestrade snapped, clearly unimpressed with this wretched little specimen of humanity, "…things are as they were, but you neither noticed nor cared. The late Miss Oakwood was the victim of a particularly cold and vicious murderer."

A faint squeak from Hubert Oakwood brought Lestrade to his senses. He turned to where the man had slumped in his chair in shock. "I am sorry, sir, I should have been more tactful about it."

Oakwood waved a hand. "I am not sure there is a way to be tactful about such a thing, Inspector," he said weakly. Oakwood straightened in his chair. "But it does make sense of a few things that my mother noticed."

"And they were?" Lestrade asked.

"Mother commented that there was no sign of anything containing poison. No laudanum bottle or anything like that. She also noted that Aunt Beatrice's favourite brooch was missing. Aunt Bea always wore an onyx cameo of the Greek goddess Athena at her throat. She wasn't wearing it when she was found, and it wasn't in her jewellery box."

"You mother is indeed an astute and observant woman," Holmes noted. "May I ask one more thing?"

"Certainly," Oakwood replied.

"Where is your aunt's body?"

"Still at the mortuary. I was given to understand by the police that we would get it back for burial eventually. Apparently, *suicides* are not high priority."

The bitterness in the young man's tone was apparent.

Lestrade laid a hand on Oakwood's shoulder. "But murder victims are. I will see to it that the good lady is released as soon as possible."

"Thank you, Inspector," Oakwood said gratefully.

Reverend Little oozed forward, eager to make up for his earlier mistakes. "Perhaps we could discuss the funeral now that I am here?"

Hubert Oakwood turned on the man, making him flinch back. "I don't want you even near my aunt's funeral," Oakwood snarled. "You who were so quick to jump to conclusions and then to judgment!" He turned to Reverend Thornwood. "You seem a good sort, sir. Certainly better than this ecclesiastical reptile here. Would you consider conducting my aunt's funeral?"

"I would be honoured to do so," Thornwood replied with a slight bow.

After Lestrade had obtained Oakwood's home address, we left them to it and headed for the mortuary.

The mortuary in question was the one on Horseferry Road, in nearby Westminster. There was, no doubt, one in Chelsea, but police cases were often sent to Westminster and, as Miss Oakwood had been considered a suicide, she had been sent there.

The mingled stench of old blood and carbolic acid slid out of the door to meet us. It was a vile smell, but it was an improvement on the early days of the morgues when the only smell had been that of decomposing flesh and blood. The addition of carbolic, whilst irritating to the senses, generally improved the scent and, most certainly, the hygiene of the place.

A morgue attendant escorted us to the office that the police surgeon inhabited when he was called upon. The surgeon, Dr. Thomas Bond, was in his office writing up his case notes.

We had met Dr. Bond on several cases. He was an affable man, well-liked by the medical profession, and well-respected by both the police and the legal profession. He was often called on to give medical evidence in court cases.

He listened courteously as Holmes explained the case to him. "I had not got to the body yet," Bond finally said. "I shall make the poor lady my next priority. If it is a case of murder, as you suggest, then it is imperative that the killer be caught."

Bond then escorted us into the morgue where Miss Oakwood's body was being kept in a drawer.

The lady was still fully clothed. The face was faintly suffused with red suggesting that Miss Oakwood's death had involved elevated blood pressure, most probably due to her struggle to breathe.

Holmes extracted his magnifying glass and carefully examined the corpse as it lay in the drawer. Eventually, he straightened up. "Apart from the fact that the lady had consumed shortbread biscuits shortly before her death, I see nothing else that could prove germane to our case."

"Shortbread biscuits?" Lestrade sounded as bewildered as I felt.

"There are crumbs on the lady's bodice, Lestrade."

"But why are they germane to the case?" I asked.

"I believe it unlikely that anyone would sit down and eat any kind of biscuit whilst deliberately ending their own life."

"You make an excellent point, Mr. Holmes," Dr. Bond said. "I shall send my findings to Baker Street and well as Scotland Yard."

"Thank you, Dr. Bond," Holmes said. "That is greatly appreciated."

On our return to Baker Street, we were met at the front door by Mrs. Hudson.

"You gentlemen have visitors," she told us, "I have settled them in your living room." She then hastened back to her kitchen.

Holmes and I shared a look equal parts amusement and bemusement before heading up the stairs to meet our unexpected guests.

Seated in our living room was Jonathan Harbury, who rose to his feet when we entered the room.

"Sorry to arrive without sending word. Your landlady settled us in here to wait for you."

Our other guest, an older woman with dark hair just touched with grey, laughed lightly. "That redoubtable lady was a little stage-struck, I think. Jonathan still has his formidable stage presence, and it can be a little overwhelming at times."

Mrs. Hudson did have a fondness for the music hall, so no doubt recognised him. I suspected that the only reason that Mrs. Hudson had not realised who he was the first time he visited was because he was with the Reverend Thornwood. You do not expect a retired music hall entertainer and an Anglican clergyman to be colleagues.

The lady who had spoken rose gracefully to her feet. I had noted the soft burr of the Scottish Highlands in her voice when she spoke.

"I am Mrs. Helena Wallace, gentlemen. Mr. Harbury here tells me that you want my help. I cannot believe that Mr. Sherlock Holmes and Dr. John Watson wish to contact the dead, so there must be another reason for my being here." She looked hard at

Jonathan Harbury. "This one would give me no details at all. Not even where we were going."

"My apologies, Helena," Harbury said. "But I felt it best that you should hear everything directly from Mr. Holmes, not me."

"A sound method," Holmes said approvingly. "No chance to form theories without all the data."

Mrs. Hudson entered then with a pot of tea. I realised that our guests already had a pot of tea, and there were plates of Mrs. Hudson's excellent ginger biscuits and lavender shortbread waiting on the table.

Once Holmes and I had cups of tea, Holmes began to explain the situation to Helena Wallace. The lady listened carefully and, when Holmes had finished, leaned back in her seat with a thoughtful look on her face.

"I have heard of the Loxworths, of course. I do not believe there is a spiritual medium in London who has not heard of them."

"Are they genuine?" I asked, ignoring the snort of derision from Holmes.

Helena Wallace shook her head decisively. "Decidedly not, Dr. Watson. Several things tell me that they are fraudulent, if not outright criminals."

Holmes leaned forward. "What things, Mrs. Wallace?"

"Firstly, the fact that they do not wish to attract attention. The primary reason for a medium's existence is to bring messages from the world of spirit to this one. This cannot be done if one limits one's circle of influence. The fact that they are limiting themselves to the middle classes is telling." She smiled briefly. "The rich and influential tend to be wise to the ways of frauds and thieves."

Mrs. Wallace paused for a sip of tea. "The fact they refuse admission to the Society of Psychical Research to their circle is not a red flag in and of itself. The S.P.R. makes many mediums uncomfortable and it is hard to make contact when you are nervous or distressed."

Harbury snorted. "A good many of my colleagues have yet to learn that getting good observations of spiritual mediums at work is a lot like fishing or birdwatching."

"It is?" I asked. "How?"

"You need to keep still, keep quiet, and try not to scare the local wildlife."

Mrs. Wallace addressed herself to my friend. "The thing that concerns me, Mr. Holmes, is this so-called Messenger of Death. That is one thing no medium ever does. If we were given any details about approaching death, we might say something like 'be careful when you are crossing the street,' but we would certainly not tell them they were going to be hit by an omnibus whilst crossing Oxford Street next Sunday. In any case, I have never heard of any spirit giving such messages."

"How are they delivering the messages?" I asked.

Mrs. Wallace shook her head. "That I cannot tell you, because I do not know how they work. I can hazard a guess. An educated one though, more like a deduction." The lady smiled impishly at Holmes.

My friend indicated that she should continue speaking.

"It is a matter of elimination. Table-turning is really only useful for yes or no questions. Tilt or turn one way for yes, the other direction for no. Likewise, the method of calling out letters of the alphabet and waiting for a yes or no response is cumbersome. However, they are both easy systems to manipulate."

"But they would work?" Holmes asked.

"They would work," Mrs. Wallace agreed. "But given that they are working with something they call the Messenger of Death, neither method would be dramatic enough for their purposes. I suspect that what they are using is direct voice."

According to Mrs. Wallace direct voice mediumship resulted in an independent voice speaking in the room but not issuing from the throat of the medium.

It was, according to Jonathan Harbury, one of the easiest manifestations to fabricate. "It doesn't have to be complicated," he explained. "If someone has a talent for mimicry it is easier. But it can also be done with an accomplice. Someone in the next room with a speaking trumpet to project the voice works well."

Holmes looked thoughtful. "You have both given me much to consider."

Taking the hint for the dismissal that it so clearly was, Mr. Harbury and Mrs. Wallace rose to leave. At the door, Jonathan Harbury turned back. "Before I forget, I did track down the lady I mentioned who came to us about the Loxworths."

"Did the lady have anything to say?" Holmes asked.

Harbury shook his head. "Unfortunately, the lady is deceased. Not a victim of the Loxworths, I hasten to add. She was knocked down and killed by a hansom cab whilst crossing the road. A genuine accident."

Holmes nodded and our visitors left.

"Another dead end," I observed.

Holmes nodded again. A little absently, I thought.

He eventually looked at me. "I think it is time to see exactly how the Loxworths work."

"You want us to attend a séance?" I asked.

Holmes shook his head. "Not us. Our names would scare our prey, and whilst I could conceivably go in another persona, you my friend, are not the world's greatest thespian. I am afraid you would not be able to sustain a fictional role over several visits."

I nodded my head sadly. My friend was correct. "Who will you ask to go instead?"

"I have a few ideas," Holmes replied. He got to his feet. "Come, Watson, we have messages to send and a council of war to arrange."

Chapter Twelve

The next day or two saw the comings and goings of many messengers, including a young man in the livery of the Diogenes Club, and several of the Irregulars. Amongst all the toing and froing, a messenger arrived from Dr. Bond.

Holmes read that missive avidly, then handed it to me. I scanned it quickly noting that the cause of death had been judged to be respiratory paralysis resulting from central nervous system collapse caused by ingesting *Narcissus Pseudonarcissus,* more commonly known as wild daffodil. It seemed that our murderer had more than one poisonous plant in his arsenal.

When I commented on that, Holmes replied, "As I said when we learned what had killed Amaryllis Winterbottom: This killer does not rely on chance. Mark my words, Watson, we will find that our murderer has a little allotment or greenhouse somewhere where he is cultivating these plants."

I looked back at the note and something else caught my eye. It was a postscript scrawled at the bottom of the note which read simply 'traces of shortbread biscuits found in alimentary canal.' I mentioned this to Holmes who just waved his hand dismissively. "I told you there were crumbs of shortbread on her bodice, why should you be surprised that Bond found them inside her body?"

I nodded, carefully folded up the note and put it in Holmes's desk.

The day before our meeting, Lestrade called at our flat in a state of agitation.

"What on Earth is wrong, Lestrade?" I asked.

"It is Miles Lovell. The man has gone and arrested someone claiming to have found the poison peddler. Someone at Holborn sent me a message."

Holmes grabbed his coat from the stand. "Hurry, Watson. We must prevent Lovell from destroying our investigation."

We were met at Holborn police station by another inspector, Herbert Hedley. "I had heard about your case, Giles," he said to Lestrade. "I don't think

Lovell wants to solve a crime he doesn't think exists, so much as put a spoke in your wheel."

I was aghast. "He would allow a murder investigation to be ruined, and a murderer to walk free simply from spite?"

Inspector Hedley nodded. "Miles Lovell is not a nice man, Dr. Watson. He is vicious, lazy, and vindictive. I have never understood how he got into the police force in the first place."

"I knew him when he joined," another voice spoke. We turned to see an older man coming towards us. "I am Superintendent Wilfred Mason, gentlemen. I knew Lovell when he joined. He had the promise but lacked the application. As he saw himself getting passed over for promotion, he became bitter. I saw Lovell's report and realised what was happening. I felt it best that you had someone more senior present."

"Thank you, sir," Lestrade said. "This is not going to be pleasant."

"Do you know whom he has arrested?" Holmes asked.

"A child, to my understanding," Mason replied.

"What?" I was aghast.

"Come, gentlemen, let us sort out our little problem," Mason said, and led us away. Hedley hurried away back to his duties.

We could hear the sound of a child crying as we approached Lovell's office. I saw Lestrade's lips tighten in anger. The set of Holmes's jaw told me he was as angry as Lestrade. I knew my own face was showing my anger as well.

Eschewing all courtesy, Lestrade marched up to the door and threw it open. He stood there glaring at Lovell, who gave him a startled look, no doubt surprised by Lestrade's abrupt entrance.

Curled up in a corner of the office was a small, dark-haired, boy who was crying so hard, he had not even noticed our arrival. Holmes hastened across to him.

Lestrade's voice was laden with disgust, "You cannot admit you made a mistake, so you try to sabotage an ongoing investigation by arresting a child. You wretched excuse for a police officer."

"The boy was selling poisons. I caught him myself. There they are!" Lovell pointed to a tatty little basket sitting on his desk. He sneered at Lestrade. "You and your stupid little theories."

I walked across to the basket. The sad little basket contained carefully arranged bundles of weeds. I noted dandelions, chickweed, garlic mustard, and something that looked a little like parsley. I removed that bundle to look at it more closely.

Holmes joined me, with the lad clinging to his side. "*Aethusa Cynapium*, also known as Fool's Parsley. Poisonous, but rarely fatal." He turned a scathing look on Lovell. "You abuse a child for a mistake."

"The brat is deliberately selling poison. I will see the wretched little specimen is punished for it. It's obvious he is the source of the poisons that those people took." It was clear that no amount of logic would get through to Miles Lovell. The man was in the grip of a delusional hatred.

At this point, Superintendent Mason decided to intervene. He had been standing in the corridor out of sight, but not out of hearing. "That is enough, Lovell!" His voice was harsh and cold.

Inspector Lovell gave a convulsive swallow and stared at his superior in shock.

"I have heard enough. Consider yourself suspended from duty." He gave Lovell a look of disdain. "Get out of my station. Now."

Miles Lovell grabbed his hat and coat and fairly scurried from the room.

Holmes looked down at the boy beside him. "This lad is Charles Richards. His mother has died. He has been living on the streets and thought he could earn some money by selling wild greens."

"Very enterprising of you, young man," Mason said.

The boy ducked his head shyly.

I looked at the bundle of greens still in my hand. "It is easy enough to mistake this plant for parsley. There is a reason it is called Fool's Parsley after all."

We left Holborn police station shortly afterwards and Charles Richards accompanied us. Outside the station Lestrade asked. "What are we going to do with the boy?"

"Leave that with me," Holmes said. "Come lad, let us be off," he said to Charles. Holmes turned to me. "I shall see you back at Baker Street." Then he and the boy walked away together.

The night of our meeting Holmes carefully set out seating for nine people, then, after some thought added a tenth chair. I raised my eyebrows.

"I doubt very much that Miss Taverner will come alone. Whether it is her clerk, Boscombe, or her cousin remains to be seen."

It turned out to be her cousin, Frederick Taverner, M.P. Known to most people as Freddie and to the destitute of London's East End, where he was held in some considerable affection, as "Flash Freddie."

Cynthia seated herself on the sofa and was soon joined by Dorothy Watts and, to my surprise, Mrs. Hudson.

Mycroft had arrived with Dorothy and settled himself into our most comfortable armchair.

Lestrade was next to arrive, greeting everyone affably before sitting next to Freddie Taverner.

The next guest was a bit of a surprise, but not a total shock. Wiggins arrived, looking rather startled to see so many people, but considerably pleased when he realised that he was being included at the planning stage of our operation.

Our last guest, however, was a total surprise. I opened the street door to find Henry Cavanagh standing on the doorstep.

We had met Henry Cavanagh during the case that I have documented as *The Curse of Neb-Heka-Ra*. He was employed as a curator in the Egyptology department of the British Museum. Cavanagh was intelligent, personable, and quite possibly the last person I expected to be involved in this case. However, I returned his greeting and escorted him upstairs to join the others.

Once everyone had been seated, Holmes began to explain why he had asked everyone to be present.

He talked about Kitty Pappwell's visit and the death of her aunt, Amaryllis Winterbottom. Then he went on to talk about the Loxworths and the Messenger of Death, and of the other victims we had uncovered. Daphne Barthwaite's visit was mentioned, as were the gentlemen from the Society of Psychical Research. Mention was also made of the things that Helena Wallace had told us, and, finally, of the note from Dr. Bond regarding Miss Oakwood.

"We need to trap the Loxworths before they claim another victim," Holmes finished with. "That is why I have asked you all here this evening. I have a plan and, should you agree to help, you will be vital to the plan."

"Count me in," Henry Cavanagh said cheerfully.

Lestrade gave him an amused look. "It would probably be a good idea to wait and see what Holmes wants from you before agreeing in so cavalier a fashion."

Cavanagh shrugged. "Leaping before I look helps keep my life interesting."

Across the room, Freddie Taverner laughed. I formed the impression that the two men would become friends before our little adventure was over.

Mycroft cut across the banter, "Tell us your plan, Sherlock."

"Thank you, Mycroft. Before we can catch the Loxworths we need to get someone inside their circle. The only way to do that is to attend one or more of their séances. With a little careful planning that person should prove irresistible to the Messenger of Death."

"That is why I am here, is it not?" Mrs. Hudson asked dryly. "I am to be your sacrificial lamb."

"More like a tethered goat," Holmes replied. "We will ensure that you are not harmed."

Lestrade frowned. "But will the Loxworths take the bait once they hear the name and the address? Dr. Watson has mentioned both in his tales of your derring-do."

"They will, because both the name and the address will be different."

"You can give Mrs. Hudson a false name, but, as Lestrade says, the address will give the game away," I pointed out.

Holmes gave me a long-suffering look. "I did say the address would be different."

Mycroft spoke, "I believe that is where I come into this strategy. You wish me to provide a safe house for Mrs. Hudson to use."

"I do," Holmes replied.

Mycroft mentioned a street close by Covent Garden. I shall not name it, as I believe that it still serves as a safe house to this very day.

"It is in a court," Mycroft continued. "Everyone who lives in it answers to me, in one capacity or another. Once given their instructions they will swear that Mrs. Hudson has lived there for years."

"Excellent," Holmes said.

"What name shall I be using?" Mrs. Hudson asked.

"Keep using 'Martha,' as changing that will not be necessary. Very few people are intimate enough with you to be using it anyway. For a surname I thought 'Cavanagh' would work well."

Henry Cavanagh looked thoughtful. "You wish Mrs. Hudson to pose of a relative of mine."

"I do. Perhaps the widow of a brother or cousin?"

"I have no brothers, and many people know that. I did have a cousin, James, who died three years ago. His wife died before him. No-one here in London knew his wife. They both lived in Devon. But friends and acquaintances of mine know that I had a cousin who died." He looked at Holmes. "But I rather think that you knew that already."

"I had heard something along those lines," Holmes replied blandly.

Mrs. Hudson was looking a little worried.

"What is wrong?" I asked softly.

"Oh, Dr. Watson, I know it is a good plan, and these evil people must be caught, but I worry about being alone in a strange house. I also worry about you and Mr. Holmes being alone here. Who is going to cook and clean for you?"

"You will not be alone, Mrs. Hudson," Dorothy said firmly. "I shall be with you. I shall be posing as your maid but, in reality, I will be there to protect you." She looked across at her employer.

Mycroft Holmes nodded. "My brother would never forgive me if I allowed his favourite landlady to go unprotected."

Freddie Taverner spoke up, "As for here, I will send around one of my cooks, a maid, and a footman to look after the place." He looked at Holmes. "Do not worry, I shall not mention the plan. I shall tell my staff that your landlady has gone to the country for her health and that someone is needed to look after the house and its residents."

I smiled at Mrs. Hudson. "Does that help at all?"

The lady smiled back at me. "It does. I know what Dorothy is capable of. I am also sure that Mr. Taverner's people will look after you well."

"We will make sure you are not exposed and put at too great a risk," Holmes reassured Mrs. Hudson. "We shall avoid meeting here. Wiggins and his Irregulars will also be keeping watch around you. When you have something you need to tell us, send one of them to me. I will arrange a meeting away from Baker Street or the safe house."

Mycroft spoke up. "There is a tearoom four streets away from the house. It is also run by one of my people. It will be arranged for meetings to take place there."

I found myself wondering just how many people worked for Mycroft Holmes and in what capacity. It seemed to me that he had people everywhere in London, and, most probably, beyond.

Wiggins spoke up. "Don't yer worry Mrs. 'Udson. Me an' th' lads ain't goin' ter let no-one 'urt yer. Yer bin good ter us. Treated us right well. We'll watch yer like 'awks."

Mrs. Hudson smiled faintly at the lad's protestations.

Cynthia patted the older woman's hand. "I shall be there as well. I am sure Mr. Holmes," she looked at Mycroft, "…has a flat close by that I can set myself up in to watch."

Mycroft nodded.

Cynthia continued, "I need to be close by, anyway, it is part of the condition of the other part of the bait."

"Other part of the bait?" I was sure I looked confused.

"Are you forgetting, Watson," my friend said, "…the fact that every murdered woman has had a piece of jewellery stolen?"

I had to admit that I had.

"Miss Cythnia has excellent contacts in the jewellery trade. I prevailed upon her to obtain the loan of a suitable piece for Mrs. *Cavanagh* to wear."

Miss Taverner withdrew a dark blue velvet pouch from her reticule. She opened it to reveal a brooch with a peridot set inside a heart-shaped gold filigree. The peridot was cut cabochon, that is, with a smooth, rounded top and a flat bottom. It was pretty, elegant, and both expensive enough to appeal to our murderous thieves, and not expensive enough to raise suspicion if they attempted to sell it.

The brooch was placed back in the pouch and handed to Mrs. Hudson. Cynthia turned to Holmes. "I had another visit from Mrs. Barthwaite. She had been going through her sister's papers and found this." She held up a leather-bound journal book that she took from her reticule. "It appears that Miss Henfold was prone to keeping a journal. She noted down how she approached the Loxworths and their response."

My friend rubbed his hands together. "Excellent. Very well done, Miss Cynthia."

"There is something else," Cynthia said softly. "Something that Miss Henfold wrote."

"And that is?" Lestrade asked, curiously.

Cynthia opened the journal at a page that I noticed was marked with a strip of velvet ribbon. She cleared her throat, and began to read aloud in a calm, clear, voice: "There is a spirit that moves amongst us.

They call him the Messenger of Death. And tonight…tonight…he called my name."

Silence filled the room, and the meeting broke up shortly after that.

Chapter Thirteen

The next few days were spent in a frenzy of activity setting things up. Mrs. Hudson moved into Mycroft's safe house with Dorothy for company. Cavanagh was a regular visitor in his role of comforting and supporting his "cousin's" widow.

Mycroft provided Cynthia with a furnished flat across the road from the safe house. The lady who lived in it was paid to take a holiday in Margate for the duration of our enterprise.

Freddie Taverner sent around the promised staff who settled in quickly. Holmes had a running battle with the maid who disapproved of his filing system, such as it was.

Wiggins and his Irregulars settled into new haunts. They were a little nonplussed to discover that locals knew who they were, and that no-one attempted to run them off. "It ain't natural, Mr. 'Olmes," Wiggins said to my friend and I on one of his quick visits, to deliver the message that Mrs. Hudson had written to the Loxworths asking to take part on their séances, "We's used ter people runnin' us orf. Not makin' us tea. Lady next ter Mrs. 'Udson even gave us crumpets!"

"Make the most of it, Wiggins," Holmes advised. "All will return to normal soon enough."

"True enough, Mr' Olmes," Wiggins said." Wiggins headed for the door and then paused and looked back at my friend. "An' thanks fer bringin' us Charlie. 'E'll be a good un. Got lots o' ideas. 'E'll be right useful once we teach 'im th' way o' th' streets."

"It was my pleasure, Wiggins," Holmes replied. "The lad needed a safe place, and being as resourceful as he is, I felt he could not do any better than being an Irregular."

Wiggins grinned and took his leave.

"You sent Charles Richards to Wiggins?" I asked, eyebrows raised.

"Not a conventional idea of safety, I know, Watson," my friend replied. "But I would not send my worst enemy to a workhouse if I could avoid it."

I understood Holmes's sentiment. The workhouses were vile places. Ostensibly they were there to support the indigent. In reality, they were a dumping ground for society's poor who were mostly treated appallingly, as if they were personally responsible for their own poverty. Which, in the case of many of the women and all of the children, they most certainly were not. Given the brutal punishments often inflicted for the slightest infraction, young Charles Richards was definitely safer with Wiggins and the Irregulars.

I turned my mind back to the case and said to my friend. "What do we do now?"

"While we wait for the Loxworths to take the bait?"

I nodded.

"Well, my good Watson, we follow the other trail."

"The other trail?"

"The missing jewellery. Come, it is time that you and I visited some of London's jewellers."

The jewellers that my friend elected to visit were not those such as the gentleman Cynthia Taverner had borrowed the brooch from. No, the men we visited were a little more downmarket than that. These men, whilst they masqueraded as respectable jewellers, and to be fair, for much of the time they were, they also had a sideline in dealing in jewellery that may not have, strictly speaking, belonged to the people they purchased it from.

Unlike the seedy receivers of stolen goods who traded in places like the East End and across the river in Southwark, these men tended to have their premises in more middle-class neighbourhoods. Though some did have shops in areas that no sane person would visit alone.

Armed with a list of the missing items, and accompanied by Lestrade in a police brougham, we set off on our expedition.

Lestrade was gloomy about the entire thing, having dealt with far too many of the sort of man we would be visiting. The sort who could convincingly plead their innocence when their case came up to court. "What do you hope to gain from this, Holmes? We already know that the jewellery has been stolen?"

"Given that few days have passed since Miss Oakwood's murder, I am hoping that we may at least find her cameo. And even if we do not find so much as a seed pearl, if we can obtain a positive identification that a Loxworth sold the jewellery, then the case is a little tighter when we arrest them."

Lestrade refused to be cheered by this pronouncement. "We all know that some of these men would sell their own granny if they could get a good price for her. They may not be as rough as the East End dealers, but they are still unscrupulous and uncompassionate. They will not help us."

"These same men would throw the same grannies under a passing omnibus if it would save their own skins," Holmes observed.

"So they would," Lestrade agreed, "…but that doesn't help us."

"Does it not?" Holmes said, the corner of his mouth quirked up in amusement. "Threaten them with being charged with conspiracy to commit murder and I am sure even the most recalcitrant ones will sing like canaries."

"Most men would," I commented.

"See, Lestrade, even our good Watson agrees with me."

Lestrade sighed and settled back in his seat. "Perhaps you are right gentlemen. Forgive me, but I have seen far too many of this kind of criminal wriggle off the hook to be overly optimistic."

I had wondered why we were not starting nearer to Bloomsbury where the Loxworth family lived, instead of Notting Hill, which is the destination I had overheard Lestrade give the constable driving the brougham.

"Too close to home," Lestrade had said, when I asked. "Too much chance that a jeweller who is even middlingly honest will wonder why someone keeps coming in with items for sale. There are only so many times your aunty can die and leave you something in her will before even the most obtuse person begins to wonder what is going on."

"At that point," Holmes added, "…the jeweller either calls the police, if he is honest, or indulges in a little blackmail if he is not."

I nodded. Put like that it made sense to begin our search at a remove from Bloomsbury. "But why Notting Hill?" I asked.

Lestrade shrugged. "Notting Hill is as good a place as any. I also know there is at least one jeweller there that has a sideline in disposing of stolen gems."

The jeweller in question was a Mr. Harrison Millworth. His shop was tucked away in a discreet laneway not far from Portobello Road, where one of London's busiest street markets was located. Like so many of London's markets it sold fresh food and household essentials such as bed linens and pots and pans.

The shop we entered was a small, but well laid out. Carefully dusted glass cases were dotted around the interior containing selections of rings, bracelets, brooches, and necklaces. Much of it pretty, in a gaudy sort of way, but, according to Holmes, nothing of any great value.

Harrison Millworth was a quiet little man who was not best pleased to have a police brougham outside of his premises. His voice was a petulant whine as he said "I have not knowingly brought stolen jewellery. You know that, Mr. Lestrade."

Lestrade held up a hand. "Be that as it may, Millworth, you did buy the countess's pearls, and that puts you on my list."

Holmes glared at Lestrade. I could understand his annoyance. That was not the way to engage the man's co-operation.

I took it on myself to step forward. "There is someone," I said, "…who is stealing just one item of jewellery at a time from corpses." I felt the man did not need to know that actual murder was involved. "We need to find the jewellery so we can find the man. Or woman," I added.

Millworth turned his attention to me. He frowned in concentration. "That will be difficult. Someone selling only one piece at a time will not stand out. Not unless the pieces are exceptional."

"They are not exceptional," my friend added. "Simple pieces that are not too expensive to attract undue attention, and not too cheap as not to be worth the thief's while."

"Have you a list?" Millworth asked.

Holmes took the list out of his pocket and handed it to Millworth. The man took a pair of silver-rimmed pince-nez glasses from his waistcoat pocket, placed them on his nose, and scrutinised the list carefully. "I can confidently state that none of these pieces have come to me," he said finally. "There are two brooches on this list. I would suggest visiting Duncan Oulfield in Covent Garden and Roger Barbeck in Soho. Both men specialise in brooches. I would think that either of them would be more likely to be able to assist you."

Holmes thanked the man, and the three of us left the shop. Back in the brougham Lestrade extracted his list of jewellers from his pocket. Both Oulfield and Barbeck were on the list. Lestrade instructed the driver to take us to Covent Garden and off we went.

Duncan Oulfield's shop in Covent Garden was closed. A sign on the door proclaimed that his opening hours were decidedly nocturnal. I commented on how odd the hours were for a jeweller.

Lestrade snorted. "Covent Garden doesn't really come alive until the sun goes down. He will make more money from those that are around here then, than he would during the day."

Looking around me, I understood what Lestrade meant. The fruit and vegetable market was not particularly busy, but it was later in the day, and most people would have purchased their requirements earlier in the morning. There were a few people visiting the shops on the upper level of the market, but it seemed that the day's bustle was winding down.

Lestrade gestured up the street to where the Covent Garden Theatre dominated the thoroughfare, sitting incongruously opposite the Bow Street Magistrates Court. "When that opens tonight, along with the Theatre Royal just down there," Lestrade pointed down the street, "…then this area will be crawling with people who are out for an evening's pleasure, and that is quite likely to involve buying a trinket for their lady-friend."

I nodded my head in understanding. Many men frequented the stage-doors of both the Covent Garden Theatre and the Theatre Royal hoping to capture the attention of one of the actresses or chorus girls. The position of Oulfield's shop meant that men could purchase something pretty at a reasonable price that might help them gain a girl's attention. The girls could not take money as such an action would get them fired for prostitution. But the "gift" of a modest piece of jewellery was something else. When times became tough the brooch, or earrings, or necklace could be sold or pawned. It was a sordid way of life, any way you looked at it.

We got back into the brougham and weaved our way around the edge of what had been the notorious slum of St. Giles. It was said that police officers had refused to patrol there alone. They always went in groups of three or more. Much of St. Giles had been destroyed when the New Oxford Road had been constructed, but enough of the slum remained to make me glad that we were travelling in daylight.

Soho was an area renowned for its small music halls, theatres, and brothels. It had an extremely large population for so small an area. Roger Barbeck's shop was located in a laneway off Berwick Street, his nearest neighbours being a music hall whose posters showed that its shows were clearly not suitable for children, a coffee shop, and, of all things, an antiquarian bookseller.

Mr. Barbeck's shop was open. It was clear that Mr. Millworth had been correct when he said the man specialised in brooches. There were several display cases that held necklaces and bracelets, but the majority of items to be seen were brooches. Pretty, whimsical, occasionally downright ugly; there were hundreds of different items on display.

The proprietor was not pleased to see us, but he hid it considerably better than Harrison Millworth had. Barbeck listened carefully to what Lestrade and Holmes had to say and then took the list of stolen items from Holmes. He got to the end of the list and handed it back with a sigh. "Wait here, please, gentlemen."

Barbeck disappeared into a back room and reappeared with a ledger tucked under his arm and carrying a velvet pouch similar to the one that Miss Taverner had given Mrs. Hudson. Undoing the pouch he tipped an item into Lestrade's hand. It was an onyx cameo. The goddess Athena looked resolutely to the right, whilst the owl on her shoulder stared straight out at the world in, what appeared to be, a somewhat judgemental fashion. The setting around the cameo was a delicate filagree in the shape of an olive wreath.

I recalled that the olive tree was said to be sacred to Athena and her gift to the Athenian people.

"I brought this three days ago." Barbeck set the ledger down on the counter. "Since the misunderstanding that almost saw me in jail, I keep a ledger of my purchases." He opened the book and pointed out an entry. "I bought this from a Mr. Simon Everard. He said the brooch had belonged to his mother. Mr. Everard did not demure when I asked for his personal details for my purchase ledger and freely gave an address in Chelsea."

I looked at the ledger. The address seemed familiar. Then it hit me. The man had used Beatrice Oakwood's address as his own. The callousness of this killer made the bile rise in my throat. From the low growl that came from Holmes, and the expletives from Lestrade, both men had also recognised the address.

"What did this man look like?" Holmes asked.

"Nothing outstanding about him," Barbeck replied. "Dark hair and eyes. Dark complexion too, might have had a bit of Greek or Italian in his background. Though his accent was not continental. There was a bit of West Country in there. I would have taken him from being from Dorset or Wiltshire. Somewhere around there."

"Thank you, Mr. Barbeck," Holmes said. "You have been very helpful." He turned to Lestrade, "Give the man a receipt for the brooch. He purchased it in good faith. Perhaps we can get his money back when we catch this monster."

Lestrade carefully wrote out a receipt stating that the item was one of interest in a criminal case, as well as noting how much Barbeck had paid for it, and handed it to the man.

Barbeck folded it up and carefully stored it in his waistcoat pocket.

Lestrade put the cameo back in the pouch and placed it inside the inner pocket of his coat.

We took our leave and walked out to the brougham.

"Where to next, Holmes?" Lestrade asked.

"Chelsea," Holmes replied. "We need to get the Oakwoods to identify the brooch."

"You heard the man," Lestrade said to the constable as we entered the vehicle. The constable nodded, and the brougham trotted briskly away from sordid Soho.

The trip to Chelsea was made in silence. All three of us ruminating on the callousness and the sheer bravado of the killer.

The house bore all the marks of grief. A mourning wreath hung on the door and the curtains were all drawn against the outside world.

Hubert Oakwood was a little surprised when we knocked on the door of the house where he lived with his parents. He invited us in and escorted us into a neat little parlour, before hastening to fetch his mother.

Millicent Oakwood was a charming lady of late middle years. Blonde hair that was fading towards mouse was arranged in a tidy chignon at the back of her head. She nodded gravely at each of us as her son introduced us.

Arranging herself on one of the comfortable armchairs she gestured for us to be seated. "I take it there is news regarding my sister-in-law's murder."

"There is, ma'am," Holmes said, clearly appreciating the fact that he did not have to beat around the bush with this lady. "Lestrade, if you would be so kind."

Lestrade withdrew the pouch from his pocket. He did not have to say a word. The moment the brooch fell into his palm both Oakwoods let out gasps.

"Aunt Bea's cameo!" Hubert exclaimed.

"I knew it had been stolen!" his mother chimed in. "Where did you gentlemen find it?"

"In the establishment of a jeweller in Soho," Lestrade said.

"The man purchased it in good faith," Holmes said softly, as much reminding Lestrade of that fact as he was informing the Oakwoods.

Mrs. Oakwood nodded. "Keep it safe, please, gentlemen."

Hubert looked puzzled. "Keep it safe? But surely it is being returned to us."

"Not yet, Hubert," his mother said. "It is evidence. Is it not?" She addressed the question to Lestrade.

"It is ma'am. You will get it back after the trial."

"Are you sure there will be a trial?" Mrs. Oakwood asked.

It was Holmes that answered. "There will be. We will get those responsible."

"And on that note, we must be content," Mrs. Oakwood told her son. The lady turned back to us. "Thank you for coming gentlemen. My husband will be gratified to know that both Scotland Yard and the renowned Sherlock Holmes and Dr. Watson are hunting his sister's killer. Humphrey was very fond of Beatrice. As we all were."

Recognising dismissal when we saw it, we took our leave of the grieving family.

Chapter Fourteen

On our return to Baker Street, to our surprise, Henry Cavanagh was waiting for us.

"I have news, and I thought you might want it in slightly more concise language than Wiggins would use."

I immediately sent for tea. The maid brought it up along with a plate of slices of a rich plum cake. Taverner's cook was every bit as good a baker as Mrs. Hudson.

Fortified with tea and cake we settled in to hear what Cavanagh had to say.

"Miss Taverner lent us Miss Henfold's diary. Miss Henfold was an excellent diarist. No detail was too small to note down. We found the exact method of contacting the Loxworths."

"Which is?" Holmes asked.

"The Loxworths advertise discreetly in several newspapers. It was just a matter of tracking a recent one down. Mrs. Hudson then wrote them a letter, as

Miss Henfold had done. She received a response in the next post inviting themselves to tea the next day."

"Bad form that," I commented. It was extremely bad manners to invite yourself to someone's home in the fashion. You sent your card, if you had one, and waited to be invited.

"Country people, I would warrant," Holmes said softly. "Unless you are staying at one of the big country houses like Barrow Hill Manor, things are considerably less formal than in the city."

Barrow Hill Manor had been the country house at the centre of a series of truly dreadful crimes that Holmes and I had investigated, and which I have written about in *The Case of the Perplexed Politician*.

"Two of them came to tea. The brother, who gave his name as Edgar Loxworth, and the eldest of the sisters, who was introduced as Eileen. You could tell that they were siblings. Same general shape of face, eye colour, hair colour, and complexion. Slight West Country accents when they spoke. The couple seemed a bit put out when they arrived to find me there," Cavanagh continued. "There was definitely relief when I said that I was there only because it was not polite to allow my dear cousin's widow to entertain strangers alone."

"How did they take that?" Holmes asked with some small amusement.

Cavanagh shook his head. "They did not even notice it was a reproof." He continued, "They asked a lot of questions. Some of them seemed innocuous, but in the light of what you had told us, took on a more sinister tone."

"Such as?" I asked.

"They wanted to know if my dear cousin-in-law lived alone. Whether she had live-in staff. Dorothy had answered the door to them when they arrived."

"How did you answer the last one?" Holmes asked.

"Mrs. Hudson told them that Dorothy lived in but had a day off every week. Going every Tuesday morning to visit her widowed mother and returning on Tuesday evening."

"Cleverly done," Holmes said softly. "Setting up a clear window of opportunity." He looked at Cavanagh. "Did they take the bait?"

"They did. After a little more chit-chat, Mrs. Hudson was told that she was welcome to join their circle as there had been a vacancy. She is going tonight."

"Are you going with her?" Holmes asked.

Cavanagh shook his head. "It was made quite clear that I was not welcome at the actual séance. I did tell them that I would be escorting the lady to and from their house." Cavanagh's face set into an expression of distaste. "The woman actually tittered and fluttered her eyelashes at me, saying how wonderful it was to meet so chivalrous a man."

"Did they react to the brooch?" Holmes asked. "I assume Mrs. Hudson was wearing it?"

"She was," Cavanagh said. "Miss Loxworth complimented her on it. Saying how lovely it was. Mrs. Hudson replied that it was the last gift from her dear Jamie, and she wore it always in his memory, that when she wore the brooch, she felt he was watching over her. Edgar Loxworth smiled and called it a 'pretty conceit' and changed the subject."

We made arrangements to meet at the tearoom Mycroft had mentioned and then Cavanagh took his leave, and I turned to Holmes. "What do we do now?"

Holmes got up to head downstairs. "We do nothing. Not yet. Wiggins, on the other hand…"

With that, he went downstairs to send for the head of the Irregulars.

Wiggins had clearly been close by, because he was in our rooms within fifteen minutes. "Watcha want, Mr. 'Olmes?"

"Can you raise enough Irregulars to keep watch on a second address?" Holmes asked.

"Corse I can. There's a regular waitin' list ter join, but I only takes th' best. I can set 'Arry an' Willy ter watch. They's bin wiv me fer a good while now. They'll not let yer down, Mr. 'Olmes."

"Excellent, Wiggins." Holmes gave the lad the Loxworths' address in Bloomsbury. "I believe most activity will take place at night when they hold their séances, but I will need to know the movements of the residents during the day as well."

"Not ter worry, Mr. 'Olmes. Liz an' Jonesie can take th' night shift. Liz likes th' night."

Liz was short for Lizard and was a boy. The lad was nicknamed Lizard because he could get into all manner of small spaces just like the reptile for which he was named. I had no notion as to the boy's real name. I suspected that most of the Irregulars may have taken new names when they joined the gang.

Holmes handed Wiggins some coins. I noticed a couple of sovereigns in the mix. "Keep me informed."

Wiggins touched the brim of his grimy cap with surprisingly clean fingers. "Will do, guv." The lad nodded to me and then slipped out of the door.

The rest of that day and evening and the next morning dragged impossibly slowly. I tried to read the papers whilst Holmes engaged in an extremely noxious chemistry experiment. Driven out by the appalling fumes, I went for a brisk walk around the Regent's Park.

I returned to find all the windows thrown open and the place airing out. Holmes was waiting for me. "Come, Watson, it is time for us to visit a certain tearoom."

We walked there in silence. Both of us were worried about using Mrs. Hudson as bait, even though she was being well, if unobtrusively, guarded.

The tearoom was pretty. Two large bow windows, with a door between them, faced the street. The ornate sign above the door proclaimed the place to be "Veronica's Tearoom." A matronly woman with kind eyes and a warm smile, whom I took to be Veronica, met us at the door, and we were escorted through the shop to a curtained off room at the back. There, seated at a large table were Mrs. Hudson, Mr. Cavanagh, and Miss Taverner.

We had just seated ourselves when Lestrade was ushered in. He looked around, "Miss Watts isn't joining us?"

Mrs. Hudson shook her head. "I told her everything last night. She pointed out that a maid going to a tearoom with her mistress was a little unusual and we want to appear as normal as possible in case the Loxworths are already watching."

"As yet that is unlikely," Holmes said, "…but still possible. I think any serious observation will not occur until a victim has been chosen."

"What if they don't choose Mrs. Hudson?" Lestrade asked.

"We find someone else and try again," Holmes replied softly. "Sooner or later, we will offer them a tasty morsel that they cannot refuse."

The lady who had greeted us returned with two large pots of tea, plates of sandwiches of thinly sliced beef with mustard, and scones with a choice of plum or raspberry jam, and cream.

Once she had left, Holmes turned his attention to Mrs. Hudson. "Tell us about the séance."

"When I arrived, one of the current regulars explained the setup."

Holmes nodded. "Three mediums with two sessions per medium. No repeat visits and no family members."

Mrs. Hudson nodded. "The payment is upfront. Thankfully Miss Henfold had noted that in her diary."

"What was the cost?" I asked.

"£12 paid in advance," Mrs. Hudson replied. "No refund if you change your mind and do not want to attend more than one."

Lestrade whistled. "That is a tidy little sum."

Holmes nodded. "It works for the clientele that they are trying to attract. Too expensive for the working class. Not exclusive enough for the aristocracy, but a reachable extravagance for the middle class." He turned back to Mrs. Hudson. "What of the séance itself?"

"It is charlatanry, Mr. Holmes, from start to finish," our good landlady replied promptly.

Holmes raised his eyebrows. "Pray elucidate."

"One of the twins was the medium. If Edith Loxworth was genuine then I would not have got a message from a so-called spirit purporting to be James Cavanagh. It would have been Humphrey Hudson, and

I would have had some rather awkward explaining to do."

"Did 'James' speak to you?" Lestrade asked.

Mrs. Hudson shook her head. "Apparently the only spirit who speaks is the Messenger of Death. The others communicate by table tipping."

Table tipping, as Jonathan Harbury had explained to Holmes and I, was a laborious method of spirit communication where the letters of the alphabet were spoken aloud, and the spirit rocked the table when the correct letter was reached. It went without saying that this was one of the easiest methods for fraudulent mediums to replicate. One popular mechanism was a pressure plate beneath the table that the medium, or a confederate, operated with their foot to get the desired results. Pressure in the right spot caused the table to tilt in the desired direction.

"What message do you get from 'James?'" Cavanagh asked.

"He warned me about getting too close to his cousin, Harry. That he did not have my welfare in mind, only my inheritance."

Henry Cavanagh snorted. "I have never been called Harry in my life. My family nickname is Hal."

"Harry is the most common nickname for Henry," Holmes observed. "They guessed that those close to you would call you that. I do not think we will have to look for other bait."

Lestrade blinked owlishly at Holmes. "How did you work that out?"

"The Loxworths are already starting to set Mrs. Hudson up as their next victim. Otherwise, why try and drive a wedge between her and Cavanagh?"

Lestrade looked thoughtful. "Good point. What next?"

"Next? We drive that wedge in." Holmes looked at Mrs. Hudson. "Next séance let it be known that you are seeing less of 'dear cousin Harry.' Cavanagh will still keep visiting, but we will keep the visits short."

"You definitely think they will take the bait?" Cavanagh asked.

"Oh yes, they will most certainly take the bait," Holmes said softly.

We finished our tea with light chatter on inconsequential subjects, before the meeting broke up.

Chapter Fifteen

It became apparent that the Loxworths were running a fairly slick business when Wiggins arrived two days later with a note from Mrs. Hudson saying that the second séance was the next night.

The morning following the second séance, Wiggins appeared again, this time with a time for us to meet at the tearooms that very afternoon.

"That is very quick," I commented. "What on earth could have happened to necessitate another meeting so soon?"

"I would surmise, my dear Watson, that the bait has been taken."

"You mean the Messenger of Death has prophesied Mrs. Hudson's death?"

"Exactly! Now, find something to do this morning, if you would. I need to make some plans and the sound of you worrying about Mrs. Hudson will prove to be a fearful distraction."

I nodded silently, finished my breakfast, and took myself out of the flat for the morning.

That afternoon's visit to the tearoom was a more sombre affair. I saw from the moment we entered the back room that Mrs. Hudson was upset. Our indomitable landlady was pale, her lips set in a tight line to stop them trembling, and her hands were clasped tightly together on the table. Cavanagh sat on one side of her, and Lestrade on the other, both men clearly at a loss as to what to say or do.

My friend, who has a heart as large as his formidable intellect, sat down opposite Mrs. Hudson and reached out, placing his hands on hers. "I promise you," he said softly, "…you will not be harmed. You will not face the killer alone. I will be there, as will our good Watson, and Lestrade, and, I have no doubt, Cavanagh as well." Holmes looked deep into Mrs. Hudson's eyes. "Dorothy will have to be seen to leave on the day, but she will also be close by, as will others of Mycroft's people. You are valued and loved by many people, Mrs. Hudson. Never doubt that, and never doubt that those people will do their utmost to keep you safe and well."

Mrs. Hudson's voice trembled slightly as she said, "Even you, Mr. Holmes?"

"Especially me, Mrs. Hudson. After all, where would we find another landlady as tolerant as you?"

Holmes's sally, as poor a wit as it was, had the desired effect: coaching a small smile from Mrs. Hudson.

Holmes sat back. "Now, tell me what happened."

Mrs. Hudson took a sip from her teacup, and then a deep breath. "The séance went much as before, except that Eileen Loxworth was the medium, and Edgar was not present."

Holmes gave her a sharp look. "Edgar was present at the first one?"

Mrs. Hudson nodded. "According to another sitter, Edgar is always present at the sittings conducted by either of the twins. Apparently, the reason for it is the twins are not as powerful as Eileen and need a boost from Edgar to make contact. Hence the table tipping rather than direct voice."

Holmes snorted. "It is more likely that Edgar operated whatever mechanism is used to tilt the table."

Mrs. Hudson nodded, and continued, "There were not any messages with this séance. Only mysterious music playing."

"How?" Lestrade asked.

"Phonograph or music box," Holmes replied. "Most likely a music box. They are more easily concealed than a phonograph."

"The music stopped abruptly," Mrs. Hudson continued, "...and a deep voice rolled through the room."

Holmes leaned forward. "What exactly did it say, every word, if you can remember them, Mrs. Hudson."

"Remember them? I am unlikely to ever forget them!" Mrs. Hudson closed her eyes. "Brethren, we gather once more to call a beloved home. Martha Cavanagh! You will come with me next Tuesday!"

Our landlady swallowed convulsively, then opened her eyes and looked at Holmes. I could see the fear in them. Lestrade and Cavanagh both moved closer in their chairs. Holmes leaned forward once more, and I joined him, reaching out across the table to our landlady and friend.

"Today is Thursday," Holmes said gently. "We have plenty of time to arrange our trap. And trap him we will. You will have house guests on Monday night. This killer will not move before Tuesday. The timing is important to him. When the Messenger of Death comes calling, we will be ready for him."

We all left shortly after that, having no heart for small talk and tea.

Lestrade accompanied us back to Baker Street. I poured us all whiskies and we settled into a somewhat gloomy silence, which Lestrade broke with a short grunt. "What I cannot understand is what the killer is getting from these murders. The jewellery taken isn't valuable enough to make the game worth the gamble."

I shook my head. "The expression is 'the game isn't worth the *candle*, Lestrade, not gamble."

"Under the circumstances," Holmes said, "I think the word gamble is rather apt. Our killer is gambling with the highest stake of all: his own life. When he is caught, he will swing. But we are getting off the point." He looked at Lestrade and continued, "This is not about money. Not entirely. The money he gets from the sale of the jewellery is by way of a bonus."

"He simply enjoys killing, then?" I asked.

"You are a doctor, my good Watson. Though not an alienist, you have looked quite deeply into the darkness that lurks in some minds."

Thinking of some of the killers we had dealt with over the years I repressed a shudder and nodded at Holmes's words. I had looked too long and too often into the darkness of the murderous mind.

Lestrade sighed. He too had seen what we had seen. And more frequently, if I were honest, being a Scotland Yard detective, he saw murder at both its most basic and its most intricate.

Holmes continued to speak, "This killer is deriving much of his pleasure from the fear he generates when the death is announced. He is, no doubt, at this moment savouring his memory of Mrs. Hudson's reaction to the announcement."

"Mrs. Hudson said Edgar Loxworth was not in the room," I objected.

Holmes corrected me. "Mrs. Hudson said Edgar Loxworth was not at the table. That does not mean he was not in the room, or able to view the room."

"Something like a peephole in the wall?" Lestrade said. "That makes sense. He almost has to be the Messenger of Death."

"How do you work that out?" I asked.

"I have never known a murderer, who wasn't political, to be part of a group. They might have a confederate. Two at the most. But the more people who know, the greater the chance is of discovery. Or of blackmail."

Holmes nodded. "In this instance, I believe it is a family affair. Edgar Loxworth is the killer, and his sister Eileen is his accomplice."

"But not the twins?" I asked.

Holmes shook his head. "I do not think so. It is possible, but I think it unlikely. As Lestrade said, the more people who are involved, the more likely they are to be caught." Holmes paused. "And we will catch them."

Lestrade finished his whisky and got to his feet. "Thank you, gentlemen. Let me know how many police you want for next Tuesday and where you want them."

"We shall work out the details and get back to you," Holmes replied. "We shall want you in the house with us from Monday evening."

"I will be there," Lestrade said, and took his leave.

Chapter Sixteen

The next morning Holmes sent for Wiggins again.

Freddie Taverner's servants had become inured to the comings and goings of the leader of the Baker Street Irregulars. The cook even going so far as to make sure she had some food on hand for him to take back to the gang. Between cook and the good people living around the safe house, Wiggins and the gang were going to be sorry when this case was over.

Wiggins was not happy when he heard about the threat to Mrs. Hudson. "Mrs. 'Udson is a lady. There ain't no cause to be threatenin' ladies. We'll keep watchin' the 'ouse in Bloomsbury, an' th' 'ouse Mrs. 'Udson's in. A mouse ain't gonna get by wivout us seein' it. Yer can trust us, Mr. 'Olmes."

"I do, Wiggins," Holmes assured him. "You and the Irregulars have not failed me yet."

"An' we won't be failin' yer this time either," Wiggins said firmly. He accepted some more coins from Holmes, and then slipped down to the kitchen, before strolling away along Baker Street.

Wiggins was back the next day to inform us that Edgar Loxworth had been seen near the safe house. "'E was lookin' round th' back o' the 'ouses. Liz thinks 'e were lookin' fer a way ter escape if 'is plan goes to billy-ho."

"Liz is most probably correct," Holmes said. "Well done, Wiggins."

"Thankee guvnor," the lad replied with a proud smile.

The next few days were filled with much coming and going between Baker Street and Scotland Yard. We studiously avoided the area around the house Mrs. Hudson was in. Wiggins was instructed to let us know when the area was clear on the Monday evening, so that we could put our plans in place. Lestrade joined us at Baker Street late in the afternoon.

Wiggins arrived shortly afterwards. "'E ain't bin back since we last seen 'im," the lad reported. "Reckon 'e saw what 'e wanted an' won't be back 'til termorrow."

"You may very well be right, Wiggins," Lestrade said. "Well-observed and well-reasoned. Are you sure I cannot convince you to join the police?"

Wiggins wrinkled his nose. "No offense, Inspector, but me an' th' lads ain't what yer'd want as coppers. Get up too many noses we would. An' anyways, we prefer workin' for ourselves." He eyed Lestrade for a moment. "If you needs me an' th' lads, we'll give yer th' same rates as we gives Mr. 'Olmes an' Miss Taverner."

Lestrade nodded gravely. "Thank you for the offer, Wiggins. I shall keep that in mind. There are often places that need to be watched but a policeman is too obvious."

Wiggins nodded back and turned his attention to Holmes, who had been watching the exchange with no little amusement. "Ready to go, Mr. 'Olmes?"

"We are, Wiggins."

The four of us left Baker Street to set a trap for our prey. I only hoped that Mrs. Hudson, as the trap's bait, would not be hurt. I had a fleeting image of a tiger hunt I once went on in India, with a terrified goat tied to a stake in a clearing as we waited for the tiger, wondering if, in this instance, we would get the tiger before he got the goat.

We slipped quietly into the little house. Wiggins remained outside, sliding away into the shadows of the evening.

Mrs. Hudson was in relatively good spirits. Now that the shock had worn off, the good lady was less afraid, and more angry, than anything else.

Dorothy was present. She sat quietly in the small back parlour working on a small piece of embroidery. She looked up when we entered the room and placed her handiwork down with a self-conscious smile. "Mrs. Hudson has been teaching me to embroider."

Lestrade looked down at her work. "That is fine work for a beginner," he said.

I looked at him sideways.

"I have sisters," he responded. "I remember what their embroidery was like when our mother was teaching them. Knots, lumps, and bloodstains abounded."

Mrs. Hudson, who came in just then with a pot of tea, smiled at Lestrade's comment. "That does happen. Dorothy, however, has fine dexterity. She has taken to embroidery like a duck to water."

Dorothy blushed faintly at the praise and rose to assist Mrs. Hudson with the tea things. We discussed plans for the next day and eventually Mrs. Hudson retired to sleep, with Dorothy sleeping in the room next to her.

I stretched out on a sofa in the front parlour, and Holmes and Lestrade found other resting places. There was nothing we could do until tomorrow. Even knowing this, sleep did not come easily. I dozed fitfully until the sunlight began to seep in through the curtains at the window.

Chapter Seventeen

I was in the kitchen, with Lestrade, wondering what to do about breakfast. Mrs. Hudson was too nervous to eat, and Holmes rarely ate at this point of a case. Lestrade and I, however, both felt the need to start the day with food.

There was a sharp rapping on the kitchen door. We both froze. None of us had anticipated that the killer might come round the back. A voice floated through the door. "It's me, Wiggins. Th' other Mr. 'Olmes says that Doc Watson an' th' inspector might want a bite o' breakfast."

I cautiously unlocked the back door to find Wiggins standing there, a broad grin on his face, clutching a large basket, which he handed to me. He saluted us both and scampered away. I retreated inside with our prize.

The basket contained easy to eat food that would not require cooking or even the use of plates and cutlery. Dorothy joined us and we quickly ate slices of cold veal and ham pie, and cold hard-boiled eggs.

Once we had eaten, we tidied the kitchen and put the basket in the scullery, a place, Dorothy said, one would often store such a basket.

We joined Holmes and Mrs. Hudson in the back parlour and worked out our hiding places.

Just before nine o'clock, Holmes retreated to a small room at the top of the stairs. Lestrade secluded himself in the scullery; a position from where he could watch the kitchen without being seen himself. I hid in a heavily draped alcove in the front parlour, where Mrs. Hudson would bring the murderer. At Holmes's insistence I had brought my gun with me, and it felt both heavy and comforting in my pocket.

Just after nine o'clock, Dorothy put on her hat and coat and left the house. Looking every inch the eager maid going out on her day off. Silence settled over the house, and we waited.

We did not have to wait long. At five minutes to ten a crisp knocking sounded at the front door. I heard Mrs. Hudson draw in her breath sharply and then make her way to the door.

"Why, Mr. Loxworth!" I heard her exclaim. "What are you doing here?"

Footsteps sounded as they made their way to the front parlour. A deep male voice, with a slight hint of West Country accent said, "I could not leave you alone to brood on this day."

"The day of my death." Mrs. Hudson's voice had a tremor that was not feigned.

"Exactly, my dear Mrs. Cavanagh," Loxworth purred. "It would be most ungentlemanly of me to leave you to deal with such thoughts alone."

I heard a rustling sound. Then Loxworth's voice came again. "I have brought with me some relaxing tea. It is a blend of my own devising. I shall make you a cup and we shall talk."

"You have brought your own teapot and cup? Whatever for? I have a perfectly serviceable teapot and cups."

"This blend is special, as I said. It does not mix well with normal tea."

I managed to restrain myself from snorting at this. The only reason Loxworth carried his own teapot, and cup, was to prevent the police from discovering the deaths were murder, not suicide. Well, he had reckoned without Sherlock Holmes.

Mrs. Hudson escorted Loxworth to the kitchen then returned to the parlour. I risked a peak from behind the drape. Holmes had entered the room behind Mrs. Hudson. He motioned her to silence, and to me to follow. I slipped out of my alcove and followed my friend out into the hall.

As we entered the kitchen, Lestrade left the scullery and joined us. Loxworth was pouring boiling water into the teapot.

"That is an interesting brew you are making there, Loxworth," Holmes said coldly.

The man almost dropped the kettle, whirling around to face us, his eyes wide with shock.

Lestrade stepped forward. "Edgar Loxworth, I arrest you for the murder of Amaryllis Winterbottom, Doris Henfold, Beatrice Oakwood, Harriet Abercrombie, and others. You will hang, Loxworth, and I shall take the greatest of pleasure in being there when the trapdoor drops."

Loxworth cursed and threw himself at the backdoor. The backdoor that I realised, to my horror, I had neglected to lock after Wiggins's delivery earlier that morning.

Loxworth raced out of the door. Lestrade cursed and went to run after him. Holmes grabbed his arm with a slight smile. "Do not worry, Lestrade."

From outside I heard Loxworth give a squawk of surprise, followed by a pained grunt.

The three of us approached the door and looked out. There was a small back garden with a vegetable patch, and a small shed for storage of tools. It was also ornamented by two men I had not expected to see. Henry Cavanagh and Freddie Taverner. Freddie Taverner's face was set in an expression of grim satisfaction, and Henry Cavanagh's was a mask of fury. Loxworth was in a heap on the ground, retching.

Taverner looked at us without a trace of his usual humour in his eyes. "The fellow ran straight into Cavanagh's fist. No idea how it happened."

"These things happen, sir," Lestrade replied formally. "Nothing to worry about."

Mrs. Hudson came to the door accompanied by several uniformed police constables, who were only too happy to take Edgar Loxworth into their custody.

The whole street watched as he was dragged out of the house and bundled into the newly arrived police brougham. Following behind was a constable carefully carrying the pot of deadly tea. Just how deadly we would find out once it had been examined.

"Glad ter see yer safe, Mrs. 'Udson," Wiggins said softly from his post at the front gate. "We's missed yer at Baker Street, we 'as. Th' cook's good, but 'er food ain't as good as yers."

"There are few cooks as good as Mrs. Hudson," I said softly.

The lad grinned. "Ain't that th' truth." He turned to Holmes. "Do yer still need us, Mr. 'Olmes?"

"Yes, I do, Wiggins. Get over to the house in Bloomsbury. Make sure no-one goes in or out until we get there."

"Right yer are, guv'nor." Wiggins hopped on the back of the retreating brougham. Giving us a cheeky wave as the carriage rolled up the street.

"Why the house in Bloomsbury?" Taverner asked.

"Edgar Loxworth was not alone in the murders. He has an accomplice."

Taverner looked startled. "Who?"

It was Mrs. Hudson who answered. "His sister, Eileen. The Messenger of Death only spoke during Eileen's séances."

Holmes bowed to her. "Well done, Mrs. Hudson. Yes, Eileen Loxworth is her brother's accomplice."

Lestrade looked sour. "I wish you had told me. I would have arranged for another brougham."

Freddie Taverner slapped him heartily on the back. "Not to worry, Inspector. I have taken care of that." He pointed up the street where his own coach sat, this time with an actual coachman on the seat. A second coach rounded the corner and joined it. I looked at the driver and started with surprise. The coachman, or rather, coachwoman, was Cythia Taverner. Freddie Taverner chuckled at my response. "I was not the only one who learned to drive as a child. Cyn did as well. Come, let us go to Bloomsbury."

He escorted Mrs. Hudson to the coach that Cynthia was driving. Dorothy was already in there. Cavanagh joined them, and Holmes, Lestrade and I joined Freddie Taverner in the first coach, and we headed to Bloomsbury.

We stopped only long enough for Lestrade to send for more constables.

Chapter Eighteen

The Loxworths lived in Bedford Way off the north side of Russell Square. The street was lined with fine Georgian townhouses. The entire area around Russell Square was part of the estates of the Duke of Bedford.

To say our arrival caused a sensation was something of an understatement, especially in an area with the bohemian reputation that Bloomsbury had. Two private coaches and a police brougham, which we had picked up on the way, were obviously not a common sight in this street at this time of day. Or perhaps not on any day.

Lestrade marched firmly up the steps and hammered on the front door. The noise brought curious neighbours to doorways, and the more discreet, to windows. That is, if the twitching of curtains was anything to go by.

The door was opened by a woman whose features and complexion said she was clearly related to Edgar Loxworth. Dressed in a morning dress of deep blue silk damask, she looked every inch the lady.

I was surprised to see her answer the door. A maid would have been more usual. Then I remembered what both Holmes and Lestrade had said about blackmail. The reality was that the Loxworths could not afford to have staff. It left them vulnerable.

Miss Loxworth looked at Lestrade, and then down to where the rest of us were gathered in the street. Taking note of the constables, she tried to shut the door. Lestrade was too swift for her, grabbing the door firmly. "Miss Eileen Loxworth?"

I could see that, just for a moment, she considered denying it. "I am she."

"You are under arrest for being an accessory to murder in multiple cases."

"It wasn't me!" the woman screamed. "It was all Edgar. I knew nothing about it!"

Mrs. Hudson stepped out from where she had been standing behind the broad back of Henry Cavanagh. "Liar!"

Eileen Loxworth gasped sharply and stared at her in shock. Clearly, she had expected Mrs. Hudson to be dead by now.

Mrs. Hudson marched up the steps to stand beside Lestrade. She stood with her hands on her hips and glared at Eileen Loxworth. "You were the only one the so-called Messenger of Death came through. You knew. You went with your brother to interview prospects. You knew. You are as guilty as he is, and I hope they hang you by your pretty neck."

Lestrade handcuffed Eileen Loxworth and handed her over to the constables who bundled her down the steps to take her to join her brother. As she was hurried towards the brougham, she began to scream and cry her innocence.

"Tell it to the court," Cavanagh said coldly as she was dragged by him. "I doubt they will believe you any more than I do."

Our attention was distracted by a small voice from inside the house. "Can we come out now?" it said in a timid tone.

Startled, Lestrade and Mrs. Hudson turned back towards the doorway. Holmes and I joined them. Two other women were peeking out of a doorway into the hallway. Their resemblance to the two criminals was clear. These must be the twins that had been mentioned as being the other mediums.

However, though physically they appeared to be much of an age with Edgar and Eileen, there was a simplicity in their eyes which spoke of much less mental maturity

"Who might you ladies be?" Holmes asked, his tone gentle. He had clearly seen what I had seen in their eyes.

"And why were you hiding in that room?" I asked equally gently.

They looked at us somewhat shyly. "We're Edith and Eleanor," one of them explained. "Eddie doesn't like us to come out when visitors come."

"Except when he gets us to play funny parlour games with his friends," the other added. "Eddie has a lot of friends."

"But they only come a few times and then don't come back. It's very sad. Some of them were very nice," the first twin said, looking sad.

It was clear that these young women had no idea what their brother and sister had been up to, and that they thought the séances were a game that Edgar had thought up to amuse both them and his "friends."

"What do we do?" Lestrade said quietly to Holmes. "I do not feel right about leaving them here. They clearly need someone to watch over them."

"Leave it to me," Holmes said. He called one of the constables over and gave him the address of the Reverend Andrew Thornwood. "Please explain the situation and ask him to join us, perhaps bringing Mrs. Helena Wallace with him."

The constable shot a sympathetic look at the twins and nodded, before hurrying away.

Lestrade sighed. "That's all very well, Mr. Holmes, but we're going to be stuck here until Thornwood arrives. Mrs. Hudson shouldn't be here."

"I'll take care o' it, Inspector," Wiggins spoke up, causing Lestrade to start with surprise.

Wiggins walked up the steps and stopped in front of Edith and Eleanor. He swept his greasy cap off his head and bowed low. "Good mornin', ladies.

Wiggins at yer service. I hears yer likes games. I knows some great card games." Wiggins withdraw a grubby package from his pocket and unwrapped it to show a well-maintained pack of cards.

"I hope you're not planning on teaching the young ladies whist, Wiggins," Holmes said.

Whist was a popular card game that people liked to bet on.

Wiggins shook his head, his attention still on the twins. "Have yer ever played *Snap*?"

Both of the young women shook their heads.

"Then yer in fer a treat." With that Wiggins ushered the two females inside and closed the door.

"Well," Holmes said with a ghost of a smile on his lips, "…that takes care of that. Come, we have murderers to talk to."

As we walked down the stairs Lestrade muttered, "I think I would rather be in there playing *Snap*."

Holmes pretended not to hear, though both Cavanagh and Taverner snorted their amusement.

One of Taverner's coaches took us to Scotland Yard, whilst Freddie Taverner and Henry Cavanagh took the other coach and escorted the ladies to their various homes.

Chapter Nineteen

The next day Holmes, Lestrade, and I returned to the house in Bloomsbury, accompanied by the Reverend Andrew Thornwood and Jonathan Harbury.

Holmes had insisted on the visit, saying that the more evidence that was acquired against Edgar and Eileen Loxworth, the happier he would be when the case went to court.

The constable on guard duty at the door saluted as we went in.

Lestrade stood in the hallway and stared around. "Where do we start?"

Jonathan Harbury pushed forward. "If you will allow us, Inspector Lestrade," he gestured to Thornwood and himself. "We are familiar enough with these situations to find the rooms used fairly quickly."

It took no more than three or four minutes before Harbury returned to escort us to a room they had found.

The walls of the room were devoid of even the simplest of decoration, and heavy drapes hung at the windows. The effect was both eerie and funereal. This was added to by the simple candlesticks that sat on the mantlepiece. There was no sign of gas lights at all in the room.

Given its size, it was clear that the room had started out as a formal dining room. The room was dominated by a large, round mahogany table with eight chairs clustered around it.

Thornwood, who was standing beside the table gestured for us to sit, and to place our hands upon the table. Holmes, Lestrade, and I sat where indicated and dutifully put our hands on the table, whilst Thornwood and Harbury sat a little away from us.

"We are sitting where the Loxworths would have sat," Harbury explained.

"How do you know where they would have sat?" Lestrade asked.

"Patience, my good inspector," Harbury said, with a roguish grin. "All will be explained shortly." He sank back in his chair, rolling his eyes theatrically.

"Is there anybody there?" His voice was deep and resonant, totally unlike his normal speaking voice. "We call to you from beyond the ether. Is there anybody who wishes to speak with these gentlemen?"

Beneath our hands, the table gave a shudder and lurched to the right. I started with surprise and Lestrade made a strangled noise. Holmes merely raised an eyebrow at the other two gentlemen.

Thornwood smiled gently. "Please forgive Jonathan his theatrics. I do think that sometimes he misses the stage more than he cares to admit."

Harbury gave a chuckle. "The temptation was too much to resist." He pushed his chair back from the table. "Come and see."

Thornwood also pushed back from the table. "I trust that the house's owner will forgive us for the damage." Saying that, he withdrew a folding knife from his pocket and carefully cut away the carpet near where he and Harbury had been sitting.

We clustered around Thornwood. He peeled back the carpet to reveal a contraption consisting of two metal plates, the edges of which poked out from beneath two of the table's sturdy legs. The plates were connected to levers that were then connected to what appeared to be bicycle pedals.

"It is quite ingenious," Thornwood commented. "I have never seen a set up quite like this. Loxworth must have designed and built it himself. Pressure on the pedals moves the levers, which tilts the table."

An eerie voice suddenly reverberated around the room. "Sherlock Holmes! Doctor Watson! Inspector Lestrade! Are you ready to meet the Messenger of Death?"

I looked up, startled by the voice. Lestrade swore.

Holmes merely smiled. "I see Mr. Harbury has discovered the method by which the Messenger visited."

Harbury, who came back into the room holding a speaking trumpet, laughed. "Indeed, I have. In the room next to this is a large cupboard that backs on to the wall of this room. In that cupboard I found a stool, this voice trumpet, and a peephole."

We went and examined the cupboard for ourselves and then continued to search the house. There was nothing in the house itself, but in the back garden we discovered a small greenhouse.

Holmes opened the door and peered in. The warm scent of growing things wafted out. There was also a foul smell. Not unlike decomposing flesh.

"Good God!" Thornbury choked. "Do not tell me there is a body in there!"

Holmes shook his head. "Not a body, Reverend. That is the smell of the foliage of black henbane." He shut the door of the greenhouse.

"I think we should leave that to experts. The glasshouse will need to be dismantled around the plants, otherwise the fumes could be detrimental to those removing the plants."

Silently, we left the house, each of us sunk deep in our own thoughts.

Chapter Twenty

It was several days after the arrests, and our exploration of the Loxworth house, before we were able to gather together to discuss the case in our Baker Street rooms.

Lestrade was present, as was Mrs. Hudson, Mycroft Holmes, Henry Cavanagh, Freddie and Cynthia Taverner, Dorothy Watts, Andrew Thornwood, who brought Helena Wallace with him, Wiggins, and Kitty Pappwell, who had brought the case to us in the first place.

Andrew Thornbury gave the apologies of Donald Porthey and Jonathan Harbury. "Porthey has gone to Manchester to investigate a poltergeist, and Harbury is currently travelling to Polruan in Cornwall to investigate a medium who claims to be in communication with a mermaid."

Holmes took the floor. "When Miss Pappwell came to me with the tale of her aunt, it was obvious that we were dealing with murder. It became clear quite early on who the murderers were, but the main problem was the lack of evidence."

Lestrade and I both nodded. This had been a frustrating case. Knowing who had killed but not being able to prove it.

"We got the evidence in the end," I said. "Caught him red-handed. Has the poison in the tea been identified?"

Holmes nodded. He had brought home a sample of the tea with, if not Scotland Yard's blessing, then a quick nod of agreement, before they pointedly looked the other way. "It was a tisane containing sweet, dried fruits to disguise the taste. The poison was *Conium Maculatum* more popularly known as hemlock."

"My heart aches, and a drowsy numbness pains my sense, as though of hemlock I had drunk," Cavanagh murmured, quoting John Keats's poem "Ode to a Nightingale."

Holmes continued, "When we confronted the Loxworths with what we knew, they both caved in."

Lestrade spoke up, "Eileen was only too eager to condemn her brother once she truly realised that she also faced the hangman's rope. Edgar is a coward who, though able to kill, cannot face the prospect of being killed himself. He has named names, times, places, and poisons. It won't save him. He has killed too many people. Even he isn't totally sure how many people he has murdered."

"But for what?" Freddie Taverner asked. "Surely it was not for money? None of the victims that we know of was particularly rich."

It was Holmes who replied. "We have seen it before, as both Watson and Lestrade will attest. They get a taste for killing. It feeds something inside them. Something that craves power. Nothing makes a man more powerful in his own eyes than the ability to take the life of another undetected."

"Except he wasn't undetected," Dorothy said softly. "Miss Pappwell here realised something was wrong and came to Mr. Holmes."

"Will Eileen Loxworth hang?" Cynthia asked.

Lestrade tilted his hand from side to side in a gesture indicating maybe yes, maybe no. "That will be up to the jury. Edgar will most definitely hang. Eileen, well, given the sheer amount of murders, it is quite possible. Even if she doesn't, she will never see anything except prison walls for the rest of her life."

"We really should not be calling them Loxworth," Holmes said. "Their family name is Brown. When Edgar thought up his little scam with the séances, he changed it to Loxworth, after the ruined manor in Wiltshire near where they were brought up. He thought Brown was too plain a name for a spiritual medium."

"Why poison?" Cynthia Taverner asked.

"According to Eileen," Lestrade said, "…Edgar had always been interested in poisonous plants. He grew his own. We found a small greenhouse out the back of the Bloomsbury house with a pharmacopeia of poisons growing in it. The experts who have examined the plants say that as well as hemlock and Black Henbane, they also discovered Dog's Mercury, Foxglove, Green Hellebore, and Monkshood. As well others that they are still trying to identify."

Holmes and I had seen the greenhouse for ourselves, and I shuddered slightly at the memory of its discovery.

"Wiltshire has both chalky and sandy soil," Holmes noted. "Ideal for growing his favoured poison, Black Henbane. He brought the soil back expressly so he could cultivate that particular plant."

"What's gonna 'appen ter th' twins, Mr. 'Olmes?" Wiggins asked. "They ain't too bright. They can't live alone. An' it ain't right they be put in Bedlam or suchlike. Place like that'd kill 'em fer sure. An' no-one 'ad better suggest th' work 'ouse." He glared around fiercely.

Andrew Thornbury had told us that when he and Helena Wallace had arrived, Wiggins had been teaching both young women to build houses out of cards. There had been much giggling and hand clapping. And not just from the girls.

Mycroft spoke. "That has been taken care of Mr. Wiggins. My brother asked me to arrange it. The young ladies will be taking up residence in a sanatorium for well-bred young women back in their native Wiltshire. An acquaintance of mine operates it. There is fresh air, good food, and games to play. They will be well cared for."

Wiggins stared at Mycroft Holmes for a moment. "Yer swear it?"

Mycroft held out his hand for Wiggins to shake. "My very word upon it."

Wiggins shook Mycroft's hand firmly. "I'll be checking an' if they ain't well looked after, I'll be coming ter yer." Even though Wiggins had lived all his life in London and had probably never even been to Wiltshire, not one of us did not believe that he meant exactly what he said. Wiggins would be checking on the welfare of the Loxworth twins.

"I would expect nothing else, Mr. Wiggins." Mycroft looked around at the rest of us. "Was there anything else, Sherlock?"

"Are the twins actually mediums?" Cynthia asked.

Helena Wallace answered, "No. They are both very fey and prone to creating imaginary friends. Their despicable brother saw that as an opportunity."

"How did they get like that?" Kitty Pappwell wanted to know.

It was my turn to answer. "It is most likely brain damage from when they were born. Birthing twins needs a lot of care, and that care is not available in small villages. I am surprised that they even reached adulthood."

"What is going to happen to young Charles Richards?" I asked. "Will he remain with the Irregulars?"

"Iffen 'e wants t'," Wiggins said. "Charlie ain't got no family. 'Is pa were in th' army. Charlie don't know where. 'E went away one day an' never came 'ome."

I looked at Mycroft Holmes who gave me a pronounced put-upon look, before saying, "I shall endeavour to discover if this Charles Richards' father is still alive. Does that suit you, Dr. Watson?"

"It does indeed, Mr. Holmes. Thank you."

Mycroft waved off my thanks with a languid hand.

"Just one more thing," it was Lestrade who spoke. He looked at Kitty Pappwell, "I thought you might like to know that Inspector Miles Lovell has taken early retirement. He was given the choice of early retirement or facing a disciplinary hearing. He chose retirement. I believe he is moving out of London."

Miss Pappwell smiled at Lestrade. "Thank you, Inspector. That greatly relieves my mind." She looked at Holmes and me, and around at the others. "Thank you all for what you have done for my aunt. I have been visited by Uncle Anthony and Uncle Lawrence," Miss Pappwell said.

It took me a moment to realise that she was referring to the lawyers Anthony Smythe and Lawrence Hastings.

"They told me about your visit. I shall visit them on my way home and let them know the outcome. Thank you, Mr. Holmes, Dr. Watson. All of you. It is a comfort to know that my aunt's murder will be avenged." Miss Pappwell then took her leave.

It was a signal for the rest of our visitors to take their leave as well.

At the door, Helena Wallace paused and looked at Holmes. "I have a message from you from Violette.

She says "*Bravo, mon petit chou! Comne tu es intelligent! Bravo, bravo!*"

Holmes stared after her. Mycroft, who had not left yet, appeared shocked.

"Who is Violette?" I asked.

"Our grandmother," came the strangled reply. I was not sure from which Holmes it came.

I decided then and there that the world was most definitely *not* ready for the Case of the Deathly Clairvoyant.

AUTHOR'S NOTES

As always, I have notes. Lots of notes.

I will start off by saying that while the fictional Loxworths were fraudulent mediums, I am well-aware that there were, and still are, many honest, reputable mediums out there. I am honoured to number two of them amongst my friends. I am sure neither Angela nor Sullivan will hold the Loxworths against me.

IEDs or Improvised Explosive Devices, such as the one that injured Major Donald Porthey are not a new item. If you are ever in London and visit the City of London Police Museum at the Guildhall, they have a dismantled IED in their collection. A nasty little equivalent of a nail bomb that was to have been used by the suffragette movement.

Baring-Gould's "biography" of Sherlock Holmes claims that Langdale Pike's real name is Lord Peter. I have taken the liberty of tacking him onto the family tree of another literary detective. I am sure you can work out which one. You could say it was a whimsey on my part.

The Witchcraft Act of 1735 had a rather long lifespan. Medium Helen Duncan was the last person to be imprisoned under the act in 1944. She wasn't the last person to be convicted under the act. That was Jane Yorke who was fined £5 in 1945.

On the subject of criminal acts, suicide was a crime in the United Kingdom until 1961. The Suicide Act of 1961 decriminalised suicide. Prior to that, those who attempted to kill themselves and failed could be tried and imprisoned. Not an act that was likely to aid the poor person's state of mind.

In case you may think I have misused Portobello Road Market, at the time this book is set it was still very much a general market. It did not become synonymous with antiques until after World War II.

On the subject of possible fumes in the greenhouse, I have read a number of accounts of visitors to the Poison Garden at Alnwick in Northumberland taking ill during the tour of the garden. If people can be affected by poisonous plants in the open air, I suspect that in the concentrated confines of a greenhouse, the fumes could prove to be deadly.

A large number of books were consulted during both my plotting stage and while writing:

"The Door Marked Summer" by Michael Bentine;

"Victorian Pharmacy" by Jane Eastoe;

"Murder Whatdunnit" by J. H. H. Gaute and Robin Odell;

"Botanical Curses and Poison: The Shadow-Lives of Plants" by Fez Inkwright;

"Poisonous Plants in Great Britain" by Frederick Gillam;

"British Poisonous Plants (1856)" by Charles Johnson;

"Calling the Spirits: A History of Séances" by Lisa Morton;

"Out of the Shadows: Six Visionary Victorian Women in Search of a Public Voice" by Emily Midorikawa;

"Houdini Speaks Out: I am Houdini and You Are a Fraud" by Arthur Moses;

"Talking to the Dead: Kate and Maggie Fox and the Rise of Spiritualism" by Barbara Weisberg;

"Beeton's Book of Household Management: An Illustrated Facsimile of the First Edition" published by Chancellor Press (1982);

"Watson Does Not Lie" by Paul Thomas Miller; and

"The Victorian Dictionary of Slang & Phrase" by J. Redding Ware.

I have many people to thank.

Vince Stadon – without whom this book would have remained titleless after I discovered that my original title was almost identical to that of another book also published by MX Publishing.

Steven Smith – who supported the Kickstarter for my last book "Sherlock Holmes and the Hellfire Heirs" by paying to be a character in this book. I hope you enjoy your outing, Steven.

Dr. Andrea Williams – a good friend whose fluency in French saved me from the horror that is Google Translation.

Penny Merritt – who has saved my sanity every time I wrote myself into a corner by providing tea and ideas in equal measure.

Richard Ryan – my editor, who has taken to asking me when I am sending him a new book.

And last, but definitely not least, Steve Emecz of MX Publishing, who continues to give my version of Sherlock Holmes and John Watson a home.

If you have enjoyed this book, you may enjoy my earlier books:

Sherlock Holmes and the Molly-Boy Murders;

Sherlock Holmes and the Case of the Perplexed Politician;

Sherlock Holmes and the Case of the London Dock Deaths;

The Adventure of the Bloody Duck and other tales of Sherlock Holmes;

Sherlock Holmes and the Curse of Neb-Heka-Ra; and

Sherlock Holmes and the Hellfire Heirs.

All are available directly from MX Publishing, and from most online book stores.

www.ingramcontent.com/pod-product-compliance
Ingram Content Group UK Ltd.
Pitfield, Milton Keynes, MK11 3LW, UK
UKHW022138020325
4813UKWH00003B/19